A TOR DOUBLE

ACTION WESTERN

**Look for Tor Double Action Westerns
from these authors:**

MAX BRAND
ZANE GREY
LEWIS B. PATTEN
WAYNE D. OVERHOLSER
CLAY FISHER
FRANK BONHAM
OWEN WISTER
STEVE FRAZEE
HARRY SINCLAIR DRAGO
JOHN PRESCOTT
WILL HENRY
W. C. TUTTLE

W.C. Tuttle

TROUBLE AT WAR EAGLE

THE REDHEAD OF AZTEC WELLS

TOR ®

A TOM DOHERTY ASSOCIATES BOOK
NEW YORK

TROUBLE AT WAR EAGLE

Copyright © 1950 by Short Stories, Inc.

THE REDHEAD OF AZTEC WELLS

Copyright © 1946 by Better Publications, Inc.

A Tor Book
Published by Tom Doherty Associates, Inc.
49 West 24th Street
New York, N.Y. 10010

ISBN: 0-812-50888-2

First edition: January 1991

Printed in the United States of America

0 9 8 7 6 5 4 3 2 1

TROUBLE AT
WAR EAGLE

CHAPTER 1

IT WAS A NASTY NIGHT IN THE ECHO PASS COUNTRY. Since morning a cold wind and rain had swept the hills, where leaden clouds, now invisible in the darkness, had seemed to hang just above the treetops. The wind had gone down, but the rain continued.

Two riders, "Hashknife" Hartley and "Sleepy" Stevens, swathed in slickers, their hat-brims dripping, rode steadily over a soggy trail, their eyes searching the darkness for a sign of human habitation. Getting lost and wet was no novelty to these two drifting cowboys—but it was unpleasant.

It was Hashknife who spotted the faint glint of a greenish-blue light, just before they came out into a road. It proved to be a little railroad depot, where there didn't seem any reason for having a depot. They ground-tied their horses and stepped up on the platform, their spurs rasping on the weathered planking, as they entered the tiny waiting room.

The ticket window was open, a gray-haired agent, puffing on a cob pipe, looking out at them. He said, "Kinda moist, ain't it?"

Hashknife slopped the water off his sombrero and grinned at the agent.

"This kinda weather might bring on rain," he replied.

"Come in and warm up," invited the agent, opening the door.

They walked in, where a potbellied stove glowed a bright cherry from its load of burning coal.

"This is shore homey," declared Sleepy, shucking off his slicker and holding out the palms of his hands to the warmth. "What town is this, pardner?"

"Echo Pass. Fastest deteriorating community in the state. Just exactly ten folks live here—two less than there was last year. Show me any community that has lost over ten percent in population in a year."

"Must be the climate," said Sleepy, drawing up a chair. "Where at are them other nine survivors?"

"Just around that clump of cottonwoods out there is the one saloon, one store, one post office, all in one building. Space is so valuable out here, we bunched 'em."

"We didn't know about them," said Hashknife, "or we wouldn't have bothered you."

"Bothered me? Lovely dove! I'm glad to have somebody to talk to. Sa-a-ay! Do you happen to be hungry?"

4

"Hungry?" gasped Sleepy. "Man, I could eat a recipe for tripe if it was printed on tar paper! And I hate tripe."

"Good! I live upstairs, yuh know, and I've got a venison mulligan on the stove. Been cookin' it all day, too. Looked at it a while ago and I says to myself, I says, 'Brass Hinkley, your eyes are a lot bigger'n your stummick.' What I mean, I've got a *pot* of it. Venison, onions, carrots, spuds, celery—and hot biscuits."

"Answer me one question, will yuh?" asked Sleepy anxiously.

"Why, sure—what is it?"

"What are we settin' here for?"

The agent laughed and looked at the wall clock, as he said, "I've got a train through in about ten minutes—and I've got some orders to deliver. That's about all they keep this station for is to pass up train orders. There's a lot of track north of here, and in bad weather them hog-heads have to know all the bad spots. Soon as that goes through, we'll hit the mulligan."

"That's mighty nice of yuh," said Hashknife, "but—well, you know, takin' strangers into the bosom of your family, like this."

"This family ain't got any bosom," declared the agent. "I'm the whole family. You don't think I'd keep a wife in a godforsaken spot like this, do yuh? And well anyway, I ain't scared of anybody who has a grin like the one you've got, my friend."

"Thank yuh," smiled Hashknife. "My name's Hartley."

"Mine is Hinkley. Brass Hinkley. Got the nick-name from poundin' brass, I suppose."

5

"And this is Stevens, known as 'Sleepy,'" said Hashknife.

They all shook hands, and Hinkley said, "Probably call him Sleepy, because he ain't."

"I'm awful good at it," declared Sleepy. "What's the next town, down the hill?"

"Nearest place is War Eagle—down in Piute Valley. It's bigger than Echo Pass, but shucks, we don't hold that agin 'em."

"You talk like a cowpoke," remarked Sleepy.

"Yeah, I've polished a few saddles," smiled Hinkley. "Been hammerin' brass for fifteen years, always in the cow country; so I never learned to talk English."

The train came rattling up the grades, and Hinkley handed up the orders on a hoop, yelled a greeting to the engine crew, and came back, as the tail lights faded out in the murk.

"Well, I reckon we'll tangle with that mulligan," he said, taking off his slicker.

"You speak of love," declared Sleepy soberly, "To me—"

A man came stumbling into the depot, halting at the open ticket window, rain dripping off his hat. He seemed out of breath, and perhaps just a trifle frightened. He glanced back at the open doorway, and said to the agent, "Can I send a telegram to War Eagle?"

"You certainly can," replied the agent. "Here's a blank and a pencil."

"Thank yuh," muttered the man and began writing. He seemed undecided just what to say.

"Can I help yuh, pardner?" the agent suggested.

"No!" replied the man sharply. "I'll make it."

At that moment a shot blasted from outside the open doorway. It seemed as though the man at the window merely turned to look toward the doorway, but he was sinking down, one hand grasping the window-ledge, trying to keep himself upright. But the hand slipped loose, and the man struck the floor in a soggy heap.

"Great Scott, what happened?" gasped the agent. "Somebody shot that feller!"

They ran out into the little waiting room, where the man was sprawled on his face, one shoulder hunched against the wall. Hashknife stepped over to the doorway and listened closely, but there was only the steady drip of rain off the roof. They turned the man over. His clothes were soaking wet, indicating that he had been in the rain for quite a while.

"Didja ever see him before?" asked Hashknife quietly.

Brass Hinkley shook his head. "I never did," he replied.

Hashknife picked up the telegraph blank, on which the man had penciled:

> Lank Morris, War Eagle.
> I HAVE GOT . . .

Hashknife read it slowly and aloud.

"He has got," said Sleepy.

"Plenty," nodded Hashknife.

"Is he dead?" asked Hinkley.

"He shore is," replied Hashknife. "Hit dead center. You better send a telegram for the sheriff

7

and coroner. If you've got an old tarp—or somethin' we can cover him with."

"That's right. I'll send that wire first."

They went back into the office, where Hashknife
asked, "Is the sheriff at War Eagle?"

Hinkley shook his head, "No, that's over in Piute.
Our sheriff is at Red Bank. Name is Charley Holt."

He tapped out the message, closed his key, and
remarked, "I'm all goosepimples, don'tcha know
it."

"It would give 'em to anybody," said Hashknife. "Do you know who Lank Morris is?"

"No, I—wait a minute! Lank Morris is the
sheriff at War Eagle, of course! I was excited, I
reckon. Now, I wonder why he was sendin' a wire
to Lank Morris?"

"I hate to interrupt," said Sleepy, "but couldn't
we discuss things over that mulligan?"

"We sure can. I'll get that tarp for the body
right now."

"And lock the door," added Hashknife.

"I can't—there's no key for it. Nobody would
touch a body, anyway. Be right with yuh."

Brass Hinkley's mulligan was a great success,
and when they pushed away from the table,
Sleepy said, "No matter what I eat from now
on, I'll never forget that mulligan."

A telegraph sounder began ticking over on a table near the bunk. Seemingly, Hinkley paid no attention, but when it stopped he said, "The sheriff
will be here about midnight on Number Seven."

He walked over and quickly acknowledged the
receipt of the wire. They sat down, after clearing

away the dishes, and Hashknife asked about cattle conditions in that range.

"We ship quite a lot from here," said Hinkley. "The HEH and the Double O are the biggest spreads, and we've got two or three small ones."

"How about Piute Valley?" asked Sleepy.

"Some big spreads over there," replied Hinkley. "I don't know much about the valley, except that they're feudin' quite a lot. Couple big outfits barkin' at each other a lot of the time, each one accusin' the other of rustlin'."

"Sounds interestin'," remarked Hashknife, stretching his long legs, as he manufactured a cigarette with his unusually long fingers.

Sleepy looked sharply at Hashknife, but said nothing. Interesting? Cattle outfits feuding, accusing each other of rustling. Sleepy drew a deep breath and shifted in his chair.

Hashknife Hartley, inches over six feet in height, lean as a greyhound, the lamplight etching the lines on his lean face, his gray eyes somber, as he rolled a smoke. Few men ever forgot those eyes, especially if they were on the wrong side of the law. Bad men had looked into Hashknife's eyes—and forgot how to lie.

Hashknife, christened Henry, came from the Milk River country in Montana, where his father had been a range minister of the Gospel. One of a large family, he was obliged to go to work at an early age, and being one of the race which won't stay still, he drifted down into the ranges of the Southwest, where he met Sleepy Stevens, also from the Northwest—Idaho. Sleepy had drifting blood in his veins, too, and they teamed up to find out what might be seen on the other side of the hill.

Finances bothered them not at all. When their funds ran low, they went to work long enough to replenish their needs. No job kept them long. Both of them were top-hand cowboys, but the lure of distant hills kept them forever on the move.

Their services were always in demand by cattlemen's associations and other law-enforcing organizations, but neither of them cared to take the many jobs offered. Hashknife, with his thorough knowledge of the cattle country, plus an analytical mind, solved range mysteries, when the law failed completely. Sleepy did not analyze anything. Just under six feet in height, broad of shoulder, slightly bowlegged, he was always ready for a laugh or a fight, and in the latter—odds meant nothing. Sleepy had innocent-looking blue eyes, nested in grin-wrinkles, and he seemed to be forever laughing at the world.

The talk drifted to sheep versus cattle, and Brass Hinkley, who had the usual cowman's aversion to "woolies," said that Piute Valley had always been afraid of sheep. Hinkley said, "There's so much open range over there that if the sheep ever get a foothold all the cowpokes in Piute Valley can't drive 'em out. They keep some rim-riders on the job all the time, but how can yuh tell that some saddle-slicker wouldn't take sheep money—and keep on goin'?"

"They've done it before," smiled Hashknife.

"What can yuh expect?" queried Hinkley. "A

few hundred dollars looks awful big to a forty-a-month cowpoke."

About ten minutes before Number 7 was due, they went down into the office, and out into the little waiting room. Here they stopped and looked blankly at each other.

The body was gone! There was the blood-spot where it had lain—but that was all.

"That's the first corpse I ever lost," exclaimed Hinkley.

"Well, don't mourn yore loss," advised Sleepy. "It's been done before."

"But why?" asked Hinkley weakly. "You—you can't use a dead man for anythin'—except buryin'."

"That's an idea," said Sleepy. "Look for a man who is startin' a graveyard."

Hashknife went over to the doorway, looking out at the drifting rain. From the north came the long-drawn wail of a locomotive whistle. Hinkley said, "The sheriff will be sore, I suppose."

"The sheriff will be glad," corrected Hashknife. "It will save him a lot of bother."

Sheriff Holt dropped off the train and came into the depot. He knew Brass Hinkley, who said, "Sorry, Chuck—but he got away."

"Got away?" queried the sheriff. "What do yuh mean, Brass?"

Hinkley explained just what happened, but did not mention the telegram. The sheriff looked at the bloodstain on the floor, and then looked quizzically at Hashknife and Sleepy. Hinkley lost no time in introducing them. Chuck Holt looked keenly at Hashknife and said:

"So yuh're Hashknife Hartley, eh?"

"Do you recognize the name?" asked Hinkley. "I thought there was somethin' familiar about it."

"I've heard of him," said the sheriff quietly. "How come yuh're in Echo Pass, Hartley?"

"Blew in in the storm."

"Uh-huh. How would you describe the feller who yuh say got killed tonight?"

Hashknife smiled slowly and shook his head.

"I can't tell yuh much, Sheriff. Maybe thirty years of age, not too tall, kinda skinny. Needed a haircut and a shave. Must have been bow-legged, 'cause his heels were worn off on the outside edges, and he tied his gun down."

"I didn't notice anythin' like that," said Hinkley.

"All right, what did you see?" queried the sheriff.

"A dead man," replied Hinkley. "He could have been sixteen or sixty, bald-headed or long-haired, and as far as I'm concerned, he might have been wearin' slippers or gum boots. Not only that, but I didn't even see he was wearin' a gun."

"Yuh're a lot of help, Brass," declared the sheriff. "You say the man came in here, leaned through that window and wanted to know about sendin' a telegram, eh?"

"Yeah," agreed Hinkley, "and they killed him before he had a chance to write it."

"Well, that's that," said the sheriff. "Let's go over to the saloon, and I'll buy a drink."

"I'm closin' up right now," declared Hinkley, "and I could sure use a drink about the size of a washtub."

* * *

There were five men in the saloon, playing draw-poker, as the four came in from the depot. Chuck Holt shook hands with all of them, and invited them to have a drink.

One big, good-looking cowman said, "What brings yuh here, Sheriff?"

"A dead man—who wasn't dead," replied the sheriff soberly.

"Let me tell it," suggested Hinkley, and proceeded to tell what had happened at the depot early that evening.

"And he pulled out before you got here, eh, Chuck?" queried one of the men.

"All he left was a blood-spot," admitted the sheriff.

No one had taken the trouble to introduce Hashknife and Sleepy to these five men until later when Hinkley realized that they did not know the inhabitants of Echo Pass. The big, good-looking man was Bob Cole, owner of the HEH spread, located about ten miles from Echo Pass. He asked the bartender about a room for the night, remarking, "I don't care about ridin' ten miles more in this rain."

"I've got two rooms up there," replied the saloon-keeper, "and if the sheriff and these other two gents—"

"I'll double up with Bob," said the sheriff.

"Suits me," stated Cole.

"I'd like a dry spot to lay the remains," remarked Sleepy. "It has been a hard day—and at the end of it a dead man who wouldn't stay dead."

"If yuh don't mind," said Hashknife, "we'd like to be led to the room."

"Go upstairs, and there's only two doors on the hallway. You take the further one, Mr. Hartley. Yuh don't need a key—there's no locks on either door."

"I salute an honest community," grinned Sleepy.

"There ain't nothin' worth stealin' in either room," commented one of the men, "so yuh can save yore salute."

It was not a good bed, but Sleepy went to sleep almost before he pulled up the blanket. Hashknife was still awake when Bob Cole and the sheriff came up the creaking stairs and went into their room. Silently he moved across the room and put his ear against the thin partition. The two men were undressing, and Hashknife heard Cole say, "Chuck, who is this Hartley person? The name is—"

"Yore education is neglected," replied the sheriff, grunting over pulling off a shrinking boot. "Hashknife Hartley, Bob."

"*Hashknife* Hartley? Yea-a-ah, that's right. What do yuh suppose they're doin' over here, Chuck?"

"I never asked him. He said he drifted out of the rain. Maybe headin' for Piute Valley—who knows?"

"Or cares," added Cole, and laughed shortly.

Hashknife went back to bed. Anyway, it was an idea—Piute Valley.

CHAPTER 2

THE RAIN RATTLED ON THE OLD SHINGLES. THERE WAS no ceiling—only the roof. From outside came the sound of hoofbeats in the mud, the faraway whistle of a locomotive. Hashknife relaxed, slid down in his blankets, when a sound brought him to a sitting position; the sound of a shot, somewhere out in the rain.

A train was coming up the grade, and he listened to it passing through Echo Pass, rattling and clanking over the switchpoints, until the sound died away in the distance.

Someone was hammering on the front door of the saloon, banging away for dear life. Hashknife heard the saloon-keeper clattering down the stairs, and the sound of excited voices at the doorway. A few moments later a man came up the stairs and began pounding on the door of the adjoining room.

"Sheriff!" a voice called. "Wake up, will yuh? There's been a shootin' done!"

Hashknife slid out of bed and reached for his clothes. Almost at the same moment Sleepy slid out the other side, saying nothing as he groped for his shirt in the darkness.

Bob Cole and Chuck Holt were talking in the next room, as they piled into their clothes, and the four men met in the dark hallway.

"Somebody got shot," said the sheriff, as they went down the narrow stairs.

There was a light in the saloon, the door wide open, but no one was in sight as they headed for the front doorway.

"Prob'ly at the depot—I heard the shot," Hashknife said.

The depot was lighted, as they splashed through the mud and came up there. Brass Hinkley, half-dressed, was in the little waiting room, along with the saloon-keeper and a girl, white-faced, her clothes bedraggled from the rain and mud. She was pretty, in spite of her disheveled appearance, and looked about eighteen years of age. On the floor were two old valises.

"What happened?" panted the sheriff.

"Plenty," replied Brass grimly, and the girl began to cry.

Hashknife gently took her by the arm and led her over to a seat.

"You take it easy—please," he said. "We'll take care of things."

Brass led the way outside and around behind

16

the depot, carrying a railroad lantern. Flat on his back, still in the rain, was a man swathed in a yellow slicker, his sombrero a few feet away. Brass held the lantern close to the man's face.

"Good gosh!" exclaimed the sheriff. "That's Luke Neves!"

"Who is Luke Neves?" asked Hashknife.

"One of the biggest cattlemen in the country— over in Piute Valley."

"Better get him out of the rain," suggested Hashknife.

"Rain won't hurt him now," said Brass.

"He isn't dead," said Hashknife. "Hit hard— but still alive. Grab his feet—we'll take him into the office."

The girl stared wide-eyed at them, as they took their burden into the office and stripped away the slicker. Brass secured some blankets and made him as comfortable as possible.

"He shore fooled me—I thought he was dead," he said.

The sheriff turned and walked into the waiting room where the girl asked huskily, "Is he still alive?"

"Yeah, he's still alive, Ma'am. Who are you?"

"I am Laura Neves."

"Oh—his daughter, eh?"

Brass followed Hashknife and Sleepy into the room. The sheriff said, "What happened, Brass?"

"Well, I was gettin' ready for bed, when they hammered on the door down here. They wanted me to flag a train for 'em, so I—"

"They?" queried the sheriff. "Her father and her?"

"No, I—there was another man. I don't know where he went."

"Mind if I interrupt?" asked Hashknife. "This investigation of why and when can wait. What we need is a doctor. Brass, will you wire for one—and tell him to make it fast."

"War Eagle is the nearest," said the sheriff.

Brass went to his instrument as Hashknife turned to the girl.

"You can prob'ly tell this story better than anybody else, Miss Neves," he said. "Why don't yuh?"

"I can't—I don't know it all," she said. "Dad didn't want me to marry Rowdy Franz. Dad and Rowdy's father hate each other. So Rowdy and I decided to elope—come here and take a train. We rode all the way in the rain—but we didn't mind rain. Then we woke up the agent and asked him to flag a train for us. Rowdy went back to take care of the horses—and a little later we heard a shot."

"And Rowdy pulled out, eh?" queried the sheriff.

"I—I don't know where he went," she replied helplessly.

The agent came back and said, "There'll be a doctor on the first train out of War Eagle."

The girl told them where they had left their horses, but both animals were gone. On the way back with the lantern they found a hat in the mud. It had R. F. on the band inside, and Laura said it was Rowdy Franz's hat.

Brass Hinkley said, "Miss Neves, me and you are goin' over to Briggs' house and ask Mrs.

Briggs to take yuh in for the night. She's the only woman in Echo Pass—and she's all woman, I'll tell yuh that."

"Thank you," said Laura. "You have all been very kind."

After they left, Bob Cole said, "That's a mighty pretty girl. If yuh ask me—Rowdy Franz is a good picker."

It was nearly three hours later when the doctor arrived on a freight train. Luke Neves was still alive, and after an examination, the doctor said he had better than a fighting chance to live. There was no place to house him in Echo Pass; so a passenger train was flagged an hour later, and Luke Neves went back to War Eagle on a stretcher.

It was well past daylight when the train pulled out. Brass Hinkley cooked breakfast for Hashknife and Sleepy upstairs in the depot.

"I've been here two of the longest years on record, and last night was the first time I didn't sleep ten hours," said Brass. "What do you think of the deal, Hashknife?"

"Well, on the face of it," replied Hashknife, "it would seem that Luke Neves overtook the elopin' pair, and Rowdy Franz shot him."

"Is there anythin' wrong with that theory?" asked Hinkley.

Hashknife shrugged. "I said—*on the face of it.*"

"What else is there to go by?" asked Hinkley.

"I don't know. Yuh see, Brass, we're strangers here. We don't know any of the circumstances. Miss Neves says that her father and this Franz are deadly enemies. We don't know this Rowdy Franz. We don't know that he wouldn't shoot down Luke Neves, desert the girl, take both horses, lose his hat—and hightail it out of the country. People are funny."

"Yeah," agreed Sleepy, "and let's not forget that another cowpoke got blasted here last night—and disappeared."

"It was sure a good night for murder," nodded Hinkley. "Where are you fellers goin' from here?"

"War Eagle," replied Sleepy quickly.

Hashknife looked at him curiously, and said, "Well, if you want to, Sleepy—I hadn't thought about it."

"Yore father wouldn't like that," said Sleepy soberly.

"He wouldn't?"

"No, of course not. Even if he hadn't been a minister, he'd hate to think he raised a liar."

CHAPTER 3

THINGS WERE REALLY UPSET IN WAR EAGLE WHEN Hashknife and Sleepy rode into the town early that afternoon. Men stood around the doctor's home, waiting for latest news on the condition of Luke Neves, while the boys from the Forty-Four made life miserable for Lank Morris, the sheriff, who couldn't make them understand that the crime did not happen in his county.

All they knew was that bad blood between the Forty-Four and the Lazy F had culminated in the attempted murder of the owner of the Forty-Four by the son of the owner of the Lazy F. They demanded action. Clint Franz kept his men out of town, fearing a pitched battle, while he went to Echo Pass, trying to get some information about his missing son. He swore that he did not know that Rowdy and Laura Neves had even thought of elopement.

Lank Morris' deputy, "Honey" Moon deplored the situation. Honey was a pacifist, who tied his holster down. He was short, fat, half-bald and entirely bow-legged. He told Brad Higgins, foreman for Luke Neves, "It didn't happen here, Brad. We deplore murder somethin' awful in this county, but we cain't do a thing about this deal, except to feel bad."

Dobie Wall, Tommy West and Bert Higgins made insulting noises, but Honey Moon merely shook his head and said, "If Rowdy shows up, we'll arrest him awful quick, but we cain't go out of our own kingdom. If you knowed anythin' about law, you'd know that. We're awful sorry, but Rowdy ain't grist for our mill."

Sheriff Morris and several men were talking in the lobby of the small hotel, when Hashknife and Sleepy came in, carrying their war-sacks. The sheriff looked them over closely, as they engaged a room from Oscar Odom, the hotel-keeper, and went upstairs. The dog-eared register showed H. Hartley and S. Stevens.

"Where from?" asked Lank, his finger on their signatures.

Oscar shrugged. "I asked 'em," he said, "and the tall one said: 'Have you got a map of the West?' I said I had one some'ers, and he said, 'Pick out any town yuh see—we're from there.'"

"Comical people, huh?" remarked the sheriff.

"Somehow, Lank, they didn't strike me as such. But after all, they're just a couple strange cow-punchers. No cause for you to get suspicious nor mystified—far as I can see."

Hashknife and Sleepy came downstairs again and Oscar introduced them to Lank Morris.

Hashknife said, "Yuh're sheriff here, eh? I want to talk with you, if yuh don't mind."

They sat down in a corner of the lobby, and Hashknife explained about the shooting of the cowboy in Echo Pass, and handed the unfinished telegram to the sheriff to whom it had been addressed. Lank read it quickly.

"That's funny," he mused. "*I have got* . . . I wonder what he got?"

"He got a bullet through his heart," said Hashknife.

"And somebody stole the body, eh?"

"A dead man don't get up and walk away, Sheriff."

Hashknife's description of the dead cowboy only caused the sheriff to shake his head. "There's a lot of cowpokes who know me," he said, "but I can't figure anyone that might send me a telegram, sayin' that he had got—somethin'. Much obliged, anyway."

Lank Morris went back to his office, where he found Honey Moon, stretched out on a cot, exhausted from oratory. He told the deputy about the cowboy killing at the Echo Pass depot.

"Where'd yuh get all that, Lank?" Honey asked.

"From a cowpoke who saw it."

"A—a cowpoke, yuh say?"

"A tall cowpoke named Hartley—I believe."

Honey sat up, his eyes wide, staring at the sheriff.

"Huh-Hartley—a tall cowpoke—yuh mean *Hashknife* Hartley?"

"I think that's what his pardner called him—why?"

"I'll be a uncle to a hipposorus!" exploded Honey, getting to his feet. He grabbed his hat and went out of there as fast as he could travel. Lank Morris looked at him in amazement. That was the fastest exit he had ever seen Honey Moon make.

But Honey was completely composed when he sauntered into the hotel lobby. In fact, his saunter was exaggerated. Hashknife and Sleepy were talking with Oscar Odom at the hotel desk, but they both turned and watched Honey. There was no sign of recognition in the eyes of any of the three. Honey came over and looked at the old register, spelling out the names carefully.

"When we came here," remarked Sleepy, "we thought we might be enterin' a civilized town. If I knew what I know now, I'd have gone right on past. There's things that is awful hard to live around."

Oscar Odom looked blankly at Sleepy, not understanding what this remark was all about. Honey turned, leaned back against the counter and began rolling a cigarette. Sleepy shook his head.

"Somebody must have persevered awful hard to learn him how to do that," he said, "but it proves that it can be done. I saw a picture once of a chimpanzee, smokin' a cigarette. I thought that must have taken a lot of patience, but this! Why, doggone it, they even learned him how to light it, too!"

"I'm amazed that it is still alive," remarked Hashknife, and without any warning, both of them grabbed Honey Moon, and began banging him on the back. Sleepy grabbed Honey's hat with both hands, forcibly yanked it down over his eyes and ears, and then they both stepped back and leaned against the counter, while Honey battled with his hat.

"He ain't changed a mite," declared Sleepy. "Same old Honey—fightin' his hat."

"Fatted up a little," observed Hashknife, "but it becomes him, I'd say."

Honey managed to yank the hat loose, cuffed it back into shape, placed it on his head and looked them over soberly.

"If that ain't assault and battery, I never felt one," he said.

"Wait a minute!" whispered Hashknife. "Sleepy, we've assaulted a deputy sheriff!"

"No! We have? A deputy sheriff? This? Oh, no-o-o-o!"

"For over two years I've been a minion of the law," declared Honey Moon.

"You couldn't beat it—so yuh j'ined it, eh?" remarked Sleepy. "Honey, it's good to see yuh again, you fat rascal!"

They shook hands soberly.

"How many years has it been, Honey?" asked Hashknife.

"Lord, don't ask me! More'n I care to admit. I've been here more than ten years. When Lank Morris said he talked with a man named Hartley—a tall cowpoke, called Hashknife—"

"You've got a wonderful memory," declared Sleepy. "Moon River Valley. It was named after you, wasn't it?"

"After my great grandfather, yuh mean. I ain't that old. Yuh know, I've told a lot of folks about you two—and they allus said I was a liar."

"Prob'ly was," said Sleepy.

"Well," declared Honey, "whether you like it or not, yuh're here—and if I do say so, Piute Valley needs yuh."

"Just what on earth could we do for Piute Valley?" asked Sleepy curiously.

Honey Moon shrugged his shoulders and drew a deep breath.

"*Quien sabe?*" he replied quietly. "But she shore needs help. Let's go down to the office, so I can make yuh used to Lank."

"We've met him," said Sleepy.

"Yeah, I know—but not the way I want yuh to meet him."

They met Laura Neves on the street with the doctor, and she spoke to them.

"How does it happen that you know her?" Honey asked in a puzzled voice.

"We were in Echo Pass, when her father got shot," replied Hashknife.

"Oh, yea-a-ah, that's how it was. I 'member Lank sayin'—you told him about some cowpoke gettin' shot up there."

"That's right."

"Well, you boys shore get around—when there's trouble."

Lank Morris didn't seem greatly amazed to find that Honey knew the two newcomers. He said, "Judgin' by the way you went out of here, you was in a hurry to meet 'em, or get out of town."

"If I had been a lawbreaker, I'd be halfway to Mexico now."

"You mean—you're goin' straight, Mr. Moon?" asked Sleepy in amazement.

"No—but I'm too smart to be suspected. Lank,

I brought you the smartest doggone cow-country detective on earth."

"Aw-w-w," said Sleepy soberly, "yuh're just sayin' that, Honey, I ain't smart—I'm just lucky."

"Yuh're lucky to be alive," declared Honey, "and I didn't mean you."

Lank Morris laughed and shook his head.

"We don't need a detective—we need an army. I'm sure glad that Clint Franz kept his men out of town today. That Forty-Four crew are on the prod."

"Over the shootin' of Luke Neves?" asked Hashknife.

"Well, that seems to be the final straw, Hartley. They've been workin' up to it. Yuh see, Luke Neves claims that the Franz outfit are stealin' his cows, and the Franz outfit swear that Luke and his gang are stealin' Lazy F beef. I don't know where it will end. Both of 'em are great fellows. That is, they were, until about a year ago. In fact, they were good friends."

"None of the other outfits are losing stock," added Honey. "It looks like a grudge deal t' me."

"Where," asked Hashknife, "are they disposin' of stolen cattle?"

"If I knew, I'd stop it," replied Lank.

"Nobody else losin' stock, eh?" mused Hashknife.

"Like I said—" began Honey, but Sleepy interrupted with:

"It looks like a grudge deal."

"That's exactly what I was goin' to say, Sleepy."

Hashknife relaxed and stretched his long legs, as he rolled a cigarette. Lank Morris studied the tall cowboy as the long fingers shaped the smoke, and decided that Hashknife would be able to take care of himself in any situation.

"Someone mentioned sheep," said Hashknife. "Somethin' about rim-riders."

"Oh, yeah," nodded Lank quietly. "Well, I dunno. Yuh hear things—about sheep wantin' to get into Piute Valley, yuh know. There are sheep north of here—and they say the range is played out. The railroad cuts along the west rim of the valley for a long ways, and yuh *could* unload sheep at certain places, I reckon. There are rim-riders, Hartley—have been for a year. Costs money, too—but the cowmen feel safer that way."

"If you've got men yuh can trust," added Hashknife.

"Yuh know, I've thought of that," declared Honey.

"If yuh did, yuh kept it to yourself," said the sheriff.

"Maybe you'd call 'em my innermost thoughts," suggested Honey.

"Yore idea is all right, Hartley," nodded the sheriff. "A few crooks could ruin the valley. Still, I think they are all dependable men."

"It'd be worth a good many thousand dollars to a sheep outfit able to throw a big herd of sheep into the back ranges," said Sleepy. "How many of them rim-riders wouldn't take a few hundred dollars—if they had a chance. Most punchers are drifters, and most any of 'em would like to drift with a well-lined pocket."

"I've thought about that," nodded the sheriff.

"He has innermost thoughts, too," said Honey.

"I'm not worryin' about the sheep now," declared Lank Morris. "My job is to try and keep law and order. If Luke Neves dies, all hell can't stop serious trouble."

"If he lives, or if he gets conscious, maybe he can exonerate Rowdy Franz," suggested Hashknife.

"I hope he can, 'cause I like Rowdy. I've been thinkin' about the cowboy who tried to send me a telegram. Doggone it, I wish I knew who he was. He must have had some information for me, Hartley. If that shooter had waited another minute, maybe we'd know."

A tall, gray-haired man walked in, and Hashknife recognized him as the doctor who had come to Echo Pass, as he said:

"Luke Neves was conscious for about ten minutes, Lank. I took a chance and asked him if he remembered what happened. He said he suspected the elopement, and saw Laura join Rowdy. He trailed 'em all the way to Echo Pass. He saw Laura at the depot, and he saw Rowdy take the horses away. He said he was under the eaves of the depot, when he heard a noise. He said he turned his head—and that is the last thing he remembered."

"That don't help Rowdy," remarked the sheriff. "Doc, do yuh think Luke will get well?"

"He has a chance, Lank—and that's all I can tell."

After the doctor left the office, another man came in. He was tall, hard-eyed, slightly gray, wearing cowboy garb. Lank took a deep breath and said, "Howdy, Clint."

The tall man said, "Howdy," and looked sharply at Hashknife and Sleepy,

"Yuh're takin' chances—comin' in now, Clint," commented Lank.

29

"Since when did coyotes scare me?" he asked.

Lank sighed and shrugged. Honey said, "I think the Forty-Four gang has gone home."

"Who cares?" asked Clint Franz.

"There yuh are," declared Honey. "Clint Franz, I'd like to have yuh meet two old friends of mine—Hashknife Hartley and Sleepy Stevens. Boys, this is Clint Franz, owner of the Lazy F."

They shook hands soberly and Franz looked sharply at Hashknife.

"No word of Rowdy?" asked Lank.

"No," replied Franz. "If there was, I wouldn't tell yuh, Lank."

"I wouldn't blame yuh," said Honey. "After all—well, I dunno."

"Hartley and Stevens were at Echo Pass, when it happened," said Lank. "They didn't see it, of course. They did see a cowpoke get killed up there that night—but somebody stole the body."

"Yeah?" queried Franz. "I didn't hear about that one. How'd it happen?"

Hashknife explained what happened, and gave Franz a description of the cowboy, also told him about the telegram.

"It must have been somebody who knew Lank," said Honey.

"Yeah," nodded Franz thoughtfully, "he must have. Hartley, did you get a good look at the dead man's face? I mean, good enough to notice if he had a wart on the corner of his lower lip?"

"I didn't see it," replied Hashknife, "but I do remember that he had a scar that cut kinda deep into his left eyebrow."

"That's the man!" exclaimed Franz. "A horse

hit him in the face about a year ago, and the bit cut his forehead. I forgot about it."

"Who was it?" asked Lank quickly.

"Dell Meek."

"By golly, I remember the scar!" exclaimed Honey. "But who would gun down Dell Meek?"

"What was Dell doin' up at Echo Pass?" asked Lank.

Clint Franz shook his head. "I don't know, Lank. Dell quit here about two months ago. Said he was goin' to Wyomin'. I thought of Dell, when you said it must be some cowpoke who knew Lank—and Dell is the only one who has left here in a long time."

"He worked for you a long time, didn't he, Clint?" asked Lank.

"About six, seven years."

"Uh-huh. I'll send a telegram to Chuck Holt, at Red Bank, and have him find out who Dell's been workin' for up there. We might get a line on who shot him."

The sheriff and Clint Franz left the office, and in a few moments three riders drew up in front of the office.

"Now, we'll have to tell it all over again," moaned Honey.

"Fresh ears, eh?" remarked Sleepy.

"Yeah. That's Jud Gibson, Nick Enright and Tobe Hansen, the whole crew of the Circle H, owners and cowpokes."

The three men came in, rattling their spurs, grinned at Honey, and demanded a recounting of anything that had happened. Honey introduced them to Hashknife and Sleepy, before starting in explaining anything.

31

"So Rowdy is at large, Luke Neves is at death's door, and everybody is mad, except us," said Gibson.

"Somethin' like that," admitted the deputy. "You boys remember Dell Meek, don't yuh?"

"Why not?" asked Enright. "He was here a long time."

"Somebody shot him in Echo Pass last night."

"Shot Dell Meek in Echo Pass?" asked Gibson. "What for?"

"And stole the body before the sheriff could get it," added Honey.

"Are you makin' it up out of yore own head?" asked Hansen.

"Yeah, and I've got enough left to make a table and two chairs," replied Honey soberly. "Dell came to the depot, asked for a telegraph blank, started to send a telegram to Lank Morris, but got shot, before he could write it."

"Got Lank's name on it, eh?" queried Hansen.

"That's right—and that's all. Hartley and Stevens were there."

"They were, eh? Are yuh sure Meek was dead, Hartley?"

Hashknife looked thoughtfully at Hansen, as he asked, "Was Meek an actor?"

"Actor!" laughed Enright. "He was a dumb cowpoke."

"Then he was dead," sighed Hashknife.

"I see what yuh mean," grinned Enright. "But why steal the body?"

"It would seem," replied Hashknife, "that whoever killed the boy, didn't want anybody to know who they killed."

"Hartley remembered that he had a scar through his left eyebrow," said Honey. "Clint Franz called the turn on the identification."

"I remember him havin' a cut over his eye," said Enright. "Well, we've got to be driftin'. I suppose the Forty-Four and the Lazy F are oilin' up their guns for each other."

"Well, they ain't sendin' each other no love notes," said Honey.

The three men rode away, it being suppertime.

"That Nick Enright is a right nice lookin' cow-poke," remarked Hashknife.

"Yeah, he's purty," agreed Honey dryly. "He's kinda crazy about Laura Neves, too. I heard that Luke Neves kinda encouraged Nick, but I don't reckon Laura did."

"You can lead a horse to water, but yuh can't make him drink," quoted Sleepy.

"What's that got to do with it?" asked Honey. "We was talkin' of love."

"I reckon we better go and get some food, Hashknife," remarked Sleepy. "See yuh later, Honey."

CHAPTER 4

THAT NIGHT THE MEN CAME IN FROM THE FORTY-Four, swaggering around, probably very glad that the Lazy F men didn't come in. Luke Neves' condition was unchanged. The word had spread that Dell Meek had been murdered in Echo Pass, and his body stolen. Hashknife and Sleepy went to bed early, dog-tired. There had been too much loud talking, too much drinking to suit them.

The hotel-keeper told them the next morning that Luke Neves was conscious, but still in a critical condition. Later on they met Lank Morris on the street, and he had talked with Neves, who said he had no idea who shot him.

"It was Rowdy Franz," declared the sheriff, "that's a cinch. If it hadn't been, why did he pull out so fast? No, he's our man."

They walked over the War Eagle Saloon and

sat down. Few were in there, except employees of the place.

"There was plenty war talk here last night," remarked Sleepy.

"There shore was," agreed the sheriff. "I don't like it."

A rider, leading a packhorse drew up in front of the general store across the street, tied his horses and came across the street. Lank said, "That's Henry Dobbs, rim-rider for the Lazy F. Prob'ly comin' in for supplies. That's a lonesome job for a man."

The man halted in the doorway. He was as tall as Hashknife, lean as a wolf, his bat-wing chaps flapping the side of the doorway. He had a long, lean face, sprinkled with graying stubble. Coming out of the bright light, his vision was not too good. He came up to the bar, ordered a drink in a husky voice, and turned his back to the counter. Hashknife had risen to his feet, and Dobbs looked straight at him.

The rim-rider's eyes snapped wide for an instant, slitted as quickly. For a moment or two he seemed undecided, but turned, as though to face the bar, and at that moment his right hand streaked to his gun-butt. No one saw Hashknife draw, but the concussion of his forty-five shook the glasses on the back-bar. The gun went spinning out of Dobbs' hand, when the bullet smashed his wrist, and he staggered back against the bar, cursing bitterly.

Not a man spoke nor moved. It was so sudden that no one seemed to realize what had happened. Then came Hashknife's drawling voice:

"Adams, you should have had better sense."

Sleepy went over and picked up the man's gun.

"Good God, Hashknife! What's this all about?" gasped Lank Morris.

"This man is Curt Adams," replied Hashknife calmly. "He's wanted for murder in Colorado, Lank—and prob'ly others that they ain't arrested him for. I thought he was in the penitentiary."

"That's a lie!" gritted Adams. "You dirty—"

The pain in the smashed wrist was too great, and he forgot the rest of it. Hashknife said, "You better take him to the doctor and get that wrist fixed up, Lank—but watch him. I wouldn't trust him, even if his neck was busted."

Honey Moon came in, and went to the doctor with Lank and their prisoner. The men in the saloon had nothing to say, but they looked at Hashknife Hartley with a deep appreciation of his gun work.

Later that morning Clint Franz came to town, but not alone. With him were five of his men, Stub Hooker, Andy Nelson, Bob Taylor, Al Severn and Tommy Reed. The men were heavily armed, and rode with Winchesters on their saddles. Lank Morris met them in front of the office and told them about the trouble at the War Eagle.

"That's a funny deal," said Franz grimly. "So our man Dobbs is Adams, a killer from Colorado, eh?"

"Adams didn't deny anythin'," declared Honey.

"That's fine—and I hired him to guard the rim."

"Who is this Hartley guy?" asked Stub Hooker sarcastically.

"He's the man who drawed a gun so fast that nobody saw him," replied Honey, "and shot a gun out of Adams' hand."

"Maybe Adams wasn't too fast."

"He wasn't fast enough, Stub," said the sheriff soberly.

They rode on up to the front of the hotel, where Hashknife and Sleepy were enjoying the shade. The two men walked out to the edge of the sidewalk, speaking to Franz, who dismounted. Hashknife said, "Lank told yuh what happened to yore rim-rider, didn't he?"

Clint Franz nodded grimly, and Hashknife said, "I'd kinda like to speak to you privately, Franz."

Sleepy walked back to the shade with them, while the five men dismounted. Two went to the post office, three into the store. Hashknife remarked, "Yo're ridin' in strength this mornin'."

"Safer that way, Hartley. What did you want with me?"

"I want to know somethin' about Adams, the man you knew as Dobbs. How did yuh happen to hire him?"

Clint Franz looked thoughtfully at Hashknife, his lips tight, but grinned wearily and shook his head.

"All right," he said. "Dobbs and another cow-poke, named Ed Jones, came in here a few months ago, lookin' for jobs. I didn't have any-thin' for them. The Circle H gave Jones a job on

37

the rim; so I gave Dobbs the same kind of a job.
They needed work—and it's hard to find men who
are willing to live on the rim."

"It's a lonesome job," said Hashknife.

"You knew Dobbs—or Adams—before, eh?
Knew him well?"

"Well enough for him to try and kill me on
sight, Franz. Yuh see, I was the one who put him
behind the bars. Cattlemen's association job."

"Are you with the association, Hartley?"

"No, we're not; that was a special job."

"I see. Well, you got off lucky. The boys say
that Adams was very fast with a gun—the fastest
they ever saw."

"It'll take him a long time to build up speed
with his left hand," declared Sleepy soberly.
"Maybe it's just as well that he goes to Colorado,
where he won't need a gun."

"Well," said Franz, "I don't reckon his past
record was anythin' against him as a rim-rider.
It was prob'ly just the job he wanted."

"It was a good place to hide out," agreed Hashknife.

"Yeah, it would be. Well, I'll have to send one
of the boys out to the rim to tell Jones what happened to Dobbs, and take out some supplies.
That's the only way he'd find out why Dobbs
didn't come back."

"Well, we'll see yuh later," said Hashknife. "No
reports on yore son yet, I don't suppose?"

Clint Franz shook his head. "Not a thing, Hartley."

"Franz, you don't think for a minute that he
shot Luke Neves, do yuh?"

Clint Franz looked at Hashknife for several moments, his eyes squinted. "Don't you?" he asked quietly.

"He doesn't happen to be my son," replied Hashknife.

Clint Franz looked thoughtfully at Hashknife for several moments, before he said quietly:

"Thank yuh, Hartley—I needed that."

Stub Hooker came as Franz started away, announcing, "Ed Jones just came in from the rim, and the boys told him what happened to Dobbs. He said he wouldn't live out there alone, and he's goin' on out to the Circle H."

"They'll have to hire another man," said Franz. "I don't blame him for wantin' company out there."

"Has Jones gone yet?" asked Hashknife.

"Yeah—he just pulled out."

After the Lazy F men had ridden away, Honey Moon came waddling up the street, turned in at the front of the hotel, and sank into a chair with Hashknife and Sleepy.

"You look kinda tired," remarked Sleepy.

"Tired?" Honey drew a deep breath and shook his head. "No, I ain't tired—I'm disgusted."

"Disgusted about what?"

"My ancestors," replied the deputy soberly. "I never knowed before what a revoltin' ancestry I've got. Horse-thieves, killers, skunks of every description, murderers. I tell yuh I'm hurt to the quick."

"Where didja get all this information, Honey?" asked Sleepy.

"From Mr. Adams, alias Dobbs."

"Read right out of the book to yuh, eh?"

"Oh, he'd done memorized it, Sleepy—word for word. Lank got a laugh out of it, until Mr. Adams started recitin' the hist'ry of the Morris family, too. It sadded Lank somethin' awful."

"Did he do any confessin', Honey?"

"I dunno what you'd call it, but I do know that from now on, all he is livin' for is to notch a sight on Hashknife. After that, he says he won't care what they do to him."

"I probably won't either," remarked Hashknife quietly.

"I wouldn't worry about him," said Honey. "Lank's wired them officials you told him about—in Colorado. The commissioners have offered a thousand dollars for the arrest of Rowdy Franz."

"Did Lank get any word from Chuck Holt, at Red Bank?" asked Hashknife.

"Not yet. Luke Neves is a little better, but he still ain't any help. I saw Laura down at the doctor's place—her and her mother. Laura won't even listen to anybody who says Rowdy done the shootin'. But if he didn't, why did he pull out?"

"With both horses," added Hashknife.

"Yeah, that's kinda funny, too."

"And another thing," said Hashknife, "they say he shot Neves so that he and Laura could get on that train."

"Well, didn't he?"

"Does it look like he did, Honey?"

"Well, somebody shot him."

"And that," declared Hashknife soberly, "is about the most intelligent statement I've heard regardin' the incident. That wasn't a killin' situation, Honey. Luke Neves followed them to Echo Pass, to try and stop the elopement. Maybe he could, maybe he couldn't. I don't believe Luke Neves would have resorted to gunplay—and I don't believe Rowdy Franz would have shot him on sight. It sure wasn't a case of life or death. The man who shot Neves never let Neves see him."

"Then why did Rowdy run away—if he didn't do it?"

"You know," mused Hashknife aloud, "if I didn't know that Curt Adams was too dumb to have studied genealogy, I'd say he was right."

"That," declared Honey, "don't answer the question, Hashknife. That's my point in this thing, and until it's settled, I won't be satisfied that Rowdy is innocent."

"Yo're just plain stubborn, Honey," said Sleepy.

"I ain't stubborn—I'm jist hard to convince."

CHAPTER 5

A TELEGRAM CAME FROM COLORADO THAT AFTER-
noon, saying that Adams was wanted for murder
and prison break, and asking the sheriff to hold
him for extradition papers. It also warned the
sheriff to take no chances with Adams, as he was
a very bad boy.

"They don't need to worry about him," declared Honey. "They can wait till hell freezes
over, and he'll still be there."

War Eagle was quiet that evening. Mike Brady,
the saloon-keeper at the War Eagle, complained
that the feud was ruining business. He said that
Luke Neves had ordered his men to stay out of
town, until he recovered—and Clint Franz had advised his men to keep away and avert bloodshed.

Hashknife and Sleepy went to their room about
ten o'clock. It was hot in that small room, over-

looking the main street. Sleepy said, "After all, why should we stay here? This ain't even interestin', Hashknife. A truce in the feud which might last a month. Doc says that it'll be a month until Neves is able to get on his feet. Why don't we drift along, eh?"

Hashknife yawned and pulled off his boots. "Might as well," he replied. "A lot of tall hills west of here." He then went over to the door, where he took a chair and put the back of it under the knob, effectually blocking any entrance.

Sleepy grinned slowly, as he said, "You ain't expectin' company, are yuh?"

"I don't know who in the world would come to see us," replied Hashknife, "but—well, it was just a hunch."

Sleepy looked thoughtfully at his tall partner, as he said, "Anythin' special on yore mind, cowpuncher?"

"No," replied Hashknife quietly, "not a thing. I looked at the old chair, and somethin' told me to block the door."

Hashknife put out the light and lifted the blinds on the two front windows. Moonlight streamed across the room, making it almost as light as the oil lamp did.

Sleepy went right to sleep, but Hashknife sprawled on the bed, wide awake, trying to puzzle out a few things, of which he only had a few minor parts to work with. Anyway, it was too hot for sleep. After about an hour he swung his feet over the side of the bed and began rolling a cigarette. There was no noise from outside. He went over and looked down at the street, but there was no one in sight. The long hitchrack at the War Eagle Saloon was almost empty.

He went back and sat down on the bed. Sleepy was snoring loudly, and Hashknife touched him on the arm. It didn't awaken Sleepy, but he shifted his position and ceased snoring. Hashknife heard footsteps in the hallway, quiet footsteps, too, and they halted at their door. Hashknife went quietly over, almost against the wall beside the door. Someone was turning the knob very slowly. A shaft of moonlight struck the knob, causing the chair to lift a little.

"Who is it out there?" asked Hashknife quietly.

The reply was very emphatic. Two loads of buckshot, spaced about a tenth of a second apart, smashed through the door, tearing the top off the chair, and most of it going through a front window. Hashknife's reply was almost as emphatic as he fired two quick shots through the door. A man yelped, and went thudding down the hall.

Hashknife kicked the chair aside and stepped into the hallway, foggy with black-powder smoke. No one was in sight. Sleepy came stumbling out, gun in hand. They could hear Oscar Odom, yelling down in the lobby, "Help! Help! Help!"

They ran to the top of the stairs. Oscar was behind his desk, looking toward the doorway, and calling at the top of his voice.

"What happened down there?" demanded Hashknife.

Oscar jerked around and stared up at them. Several men came running in, one of them Lank Morris who barked:

"Where was all that shootin' Oscar?"

"Shootin'?" asked Oscar blankly ". . . I didn't hear—oh, that's right! What became of the man with the shotgun?"

Hashknife and Sleepy came down, clad in their underclothes, and as Oscar was too excited to talk coherently, the sheriff said, "What happened, Hartley?"

"Well, I don't know exactly, Lank, but I do know that somebody riddled our door with buckshot."

"Riddled your door? I—I don't understand."

"Wait!" begged Oscar. "I'll tell yuh what happened to me. I was settin' here, readin' when all to once a man shoved a gun into my face, hunched over and got behind the desk with me. He had a mask on his face, and he said he'd kill me if I made a sound. Another man went up the stairs, and I think he had a shotgun. The man with me said, 'Just keep your mouth shut and you won't get hurt. This won't take long.'"

Oscar paused and licked his lips, before he said dryly:

"For once in my life I kept my mouth shut."

"Scared, eh?" remarked one of the men.

"No, I wasn't—I just couldn't think of a damn word to say."

"Let's take a look at the room," suggested Lank Morris.

The charges of shot had smashed a hole in the door near the knob, and the top panel of the chair was practically shot in two. Oscar Odom looked sadly at the broken window and the ruined door.

"Here's two bullet holes," said the sheriff, pointing them out.

"I shot twice through the door," said Hashknife. "Bring the light out here, will yuh? I heard that feller yelp out when I shot."

They found a splatter of blood against the plastered wall, more along the hallway to the back stairs, and a trace of it on the back stairs.

"You must have hit him, Hartley!" exclaimed Lank Morris.

"That's right," agreed Hashknife. "He packed away a bullet."

"He did? How do yuh know he packed away a bullet?"

"There's only one bullet hole in the wall, Lank—and I shot twice."

"That's right—there's only one bullet hole. Well, he's gone."

"How about another room, Oscar?" asked Hashknife. "This one has too much ventilation—and that hombre might come back."

"Take the one next to it," replied Oscar. "They're all alike."

"I'll see yuh in the mornin'," said the sheriff, "and we'll talk over this deal. I want to know why somebody wants to kill you."

"So do I," replied Hashknife soberly. "If you figure out a solution tonight, I'll be glad to hear it tomorrow, Lank."

"I'm not askin' any questions," remarked Sleepy, as he got into bed, "but yore hunch was well founded, pardner. Man, if you hadn't blocked that door—"

"I was awake," smiled Hashknife. "He carefully turned the knob and shoved against the door. I asked who it was—and I got his answer."

"He saw he was blocked, so he took a chance that yuh might be in front of the door."

"That's right. Do yuh still think it ain't interestin'?"

"Well," grinned Sleepy, "I ain't what you'd call a changeable person, but I've shore shifted my ideas tonight."

Lank Morris left the hotel, intending to go home, but decided to see if everything was all right at the office and jail. Honey was supposed to be sleeping on a cot in the office, but he did not answer Lank's hammering on the door. So Lank unlocked the place. There was the cot, all made up neatly, but no sign of Honey Moon.

Lank hurried down the corridor, unlocked the door and stepped into the jail. Curt Adams' cell door was wide open, Adams gone. Lank ran back to the office and opened his desk. Adams' gun was gone, and a thirty-thirty Winchester was missing from the gun-rack. Lank stood beside his desk, wondering just what move to make next, when his eyes centered on a sheet of paper on the desk, on which had been printed in large capitals:

HARTLEY—YOU BETTER START RUNNIN' OR PRAYIN'.

ADAMS

Lank walked out of the office and locked the door. There did not seem to be any use as yet of sounding an alarm. He hurried down the alley past the jail and flung open the stable doors. Quickly he lighted a lantern and looked into the two stalls. His own roan saddle horse was gone, as were his saddle and bridle. A grunting sound, somewhere in the stable, drew him over to the grain box, where he found Honey Moon, all tied up, gagged and stuffed into a space too small for one of his size. In fact, Lank had quite a time getting Honey loose from the box.

Honey was entirely conscious, but had no idea what happened and was much concerned over an egg-sized lump on his head. He did tell Lank that he had gone out to see if the horses were all right for the night, and something had hit him on the head. Lank tried to explain that their prisoner was gone, but Honey only said:

"Don't clutter me with details, Lank—please. All I want is somethin' for my head, and a place to stretch out."

"He took my rifle, my horse and saddle," complained Lank.

"Who did?" asked Honey.

"Curt Adams, our prisoner. Honey, don't yuh realize—he's gone?"

"Gone?" gasped Honey. "Yuh mean—yuh do? Gone, eh? Well, why didn't yuh stop him? No, I don't mean that, Lank. I—I'm kinda confused, I reckon. Maybe I better get some sleep."

"How about goin' down and have Doc look at yore head?"

"Huh? Look at my head? What'sa use of that— he's seen it hundreds of times. No, I think I'll skip that, and get myself to bed."

"Yeah, I think that's the best idea," agreed Lank. "You go ahead, Honey—I'll see yuh mañana."

CHAPTER 6

Hashknife and Sleepy met Lank Morris and Honey Moon in the hotel restaurant next morning, and the two officers told their troubles. Hashknife read the note signed by Adams.

"I told yuh he's got his mind on yore demise, Hashknife," Honey said.

Hashknife smiled slowly. "I'm not afraid of Adams," he said. "Yuh see, Adams hasn't education enough to write that note—even if he didn't have a busted right hand. We know that he's got at least two friends around here."

"He worked for Clint Franz," said Honey meaningly.

"How is Luke Neves this mornin'?" asked Hashknife.

"Haven't heard yet," replied the sheriff. "We're goin' down there after breakfast."

"We'll go with yuh, Lank," said Hashknife. "If Neves is able to talk, I'd like to ask him a few questions."

They finished breakfast and went down to the doctor's home, where they found Mrs. Neves and Laura sitting in a buckboard. Laura said, "We were just going up to tell you—we can't find anybody around here."

"Yuh mean—they don't answer?" asked Lank quickly.

"That's right. I've hammered on the doors—and they're locked."

"That's mighty funny," remarked Lank. "Even if Doc went out on a case, Mrs. Willis ought to be home. She does all of the nursin' for Doc."

But there was evidently nobody at home. Hashknife went around the house. On one side, where weeds grew in close, there was a trash-pile near a window, and on the pile was what looked like an old shirt. Hashknife kicked it away from the pile of debris, and discovered that it was blood-stained, the blood hardened. Quickly he smoothed it as much as possible. There was what might have been a bullet hole in the cloth, and there was something in the pocket, which proved to be a folded letter, badly soaked with dried blood. Hashknife wrapped it in his handkerchief and put it in his pocket, as Lank Morris came around the corner. Hashknife showed Lank the bloody shirt, and the sheriff looked at it grimly.

"We're bustin' in a door, Hartley," he said.

They had little trouble breaking the old-fashioned lock, and went into the house. Here they found Luke Neves who was all right, but almost as curious as they were. He said husikly, and with effort:

"I heard voices last night, but couldn't hear what was said. Neither Doc nor Mrs. Willis came in to see me after that. I have no watch nor clock in here, but I could tell by the angle of the sun that it was long past morning."

Lank introduced Hashknife and Sleepy to Luke who remarked, "Laura told me about you two boys bein' at Echo Pass."

Lank said, "Luke, I'm glad yuh told yore boys to keep out of trouble in town. It makes it easier for my office."

"We don't want trouble," said Mrs. Neves quietly. "After all, it doesn't settle anything."

"One of these days it will," declared Luke Neves. "This valley ain't big enough for me and Clint Franz."

Lank told Neves about the trouble between Hashknife and the man they knew as Dobbs, and the jailbreak of Dobbs. Neves listened grimly. He knew that Dobbs worked for the Lazy F, and it seemed to worry him.

"We've got to put more men on the rim," he said.

"Your only worry right now is to get well," declared Laura.

"And mine is to find Doc and his wife," said Lank. "And the Lord only knows where they are."

They went out, leaving the two women with the patient. Honey still had a headache, and a sizable lump on his head. He and Lank went back to the office, but Hashknife and Sleepy sat on the doctor's porch, where Mrs. Neves joined them. She

51

said that Laura was preparing some breakfast for the patient. Mrs. Neves was a small, gray-haired woman, who was still pretty in spite of her years on a ranch.

Hashknife said, "Mrs. Neves, it ain't none of my business, but I wish you'd tell me how the trouble ever got started between the Forty-Four and the Lazy F."

Mrs. Neves smiled wearily, as she sat down on the steps.

"It isn't any secret," she said quietly. "It started over a year ago, when a cattle buyer came here to fill a rush order for a hundred head. He got a price from Luke. He didn't say he would take them, but he told Luke to throw the hundred head into a corral, where he could look them over.

"Then he went to the Lazy F, told Clint Franz the price quoted by us, and Franz cut that price by about ten percent, which wasn't exactly the thing to do. When the boys went out to turn our stock out of the corral back in the hills, they were already gone—and we have never seen them since.

"And when the buyer went out to look at the hundred head he had bought from the Lazy F, the corral had been cut, and every head was gone. Clint Franz swore they had been stolen and blamed us for getting even with him on the cut price. The buyer cancelled the order and left here in a huff.

"About two weeks later our best waterhole was poisoned, and we found twenty-seven head of dead cows. Since then we have lost a lot of cows, Mr. Hartley."

"And so has the Lazy F, I understand."

"Luke," said Mrs. Neves, "swears that Franz tells things like that to cover his own misdeeds."

"Were Luke Neves and Clint Franz ever good friends?"

"The best," replied Mrs. Neves.

"Who was the cattle buyer, and who did he buy for?" asked Hashknife.

"I don't know, Mr. Hartley; he never came here again."

"You think I'm pretty nosey, don't yuh, Ma'am?" asked Hashknife.

"No, I—well, I did—at first. But then—" Mrs. Neves looked at Hashknife and they both smiled.

"You don't now, eh?" he said. "But you prob'ly will, when I ask yuh if anybody has tried to buy the Forty-Four—recently?"

"Why, no—not exactly recently. About seven or eight months ago a man came to the valley, and made Luke an offer for the Forty-Four, but it was far below our price. I heard later that he made Clint Franz a price for the Lazy F, but it was turned down."

"Thank yuh, Ma'am. Just one other question— do you believe that Rowdy Franz shot yore husband?"

"I'm sorry, Mr. Hartley, but, until it is proved otherwise—"

"I don't blame yuh, Ma'am—but I don't believe he did."

Just then a horse and buggy turned off a dirt

street, and came toward the house. Mrs. Neves exclaimed, "That is Doctor Willis!"

She got up and hurried into the house. Doctor Willis tied his old sorrel buggy horse to the fence and came up the short walk, carrying his black bag. Neither Hashknife nor Sleepy knew him very well, but it seemed to them that he looked ten years older this morning. He didn't speak, just looked at them blankly, as he went past and into the house.

"Looks like he'd seen a whole flock of ghosts," remarked Sleepy.

"Maybe he has," whispered Hashknife.

They could hear Mrs. Neves and Laura plying him with questions, but they didn't seem to be getting any answers.

"We'll go tell Lank that Doc is back," suggested Hashknife. "Maybe he'll talk to Lank—but I doubt it."

As they walked up the wooden sidewalk, Sleepy said, "Why do yuh doubt it, pardner?"

"Because men don't see a flock of ghosts—and talk about 'em."

They told the sheriff of the doctor's return, and he headed for the doctor's place at a trot. Honey said, "I'm still headachy."

"Yo're a fine deputy," said Sleepy: "Let a crippled killer get out of jail the first night you've got him. We heard you said he'd be there until hell froze over."

"Can you prove that it ain't?" asked Honey.

"Aw, don't get technical," said Sleepy.

Honey sighed and rubbed his sore head, as he

remarked, "You fellers must be prayin'—I don't see yuh runnin'."

They left Honey to his sore head and went up to their room at the hotel, where Hashknife produced the blood-soaked handful of crumpled paper. He told Sleepy where he had found it, and together they tried to separate it enough to find out what had been said on it. The blood had dried on the cheap paper, obliterating much of the penciled scrawl. They couldn't find any name that was legible, but part of one page, with certain letters and words blocked out, read:

> We will .... on .. 20th .... arrange to spot cars .... old ...... mine .... handle 20 or 25 .... they tell me. It .... your job to .... area .. clear. A big .... War Eagle .... help a lot. The boss refuses to .... any longer .... it's .... go ahead .... 'em in. Have .... help you ....

That was all they were able to decipher, except for a word, here and there, but no names. Hashknife studied the soggy paper, which he soaked in a bowl of water, but the words were either blotted out, or the penciled lines had faded.

"What do they mean by the twentieth?" asked Sleepy.

Hashknife looked thoughtfully at Sleepy, as he replied, "This is the fifteenth of the month, pardner. Could this mean that they will ship sheep on the twentieth, and unload them at some mine siding along the rim? Could be. Now, what would

be a big something' in War Eagle? Maybe a fire!
Let's go talk with Lank, and find out if there is
any mine sidin' on the rim."

Lank Morris reached his office the same time
they did. He sat down at his desk and flung his
hat aside. Lank was disturbed. Honey said soberly, "That's why yuh never have a decent-
lookin' hat—throwin' 'em around thataway."

"Doc won't talk!" exclaimed the sheriff. "He
won't tell where he's been, and he won't tell
where his wife is. He just shakes his head."

"His wife is a nurse, eh?" said Hashknife.

"The best there is," replied Lank. "She was a
hospital nurse in Tucson, where Doc married
her. She's about as good a doctor as her husband
is."

"Don't *make* him talk," said Hashknife.

"Don't make him talk? Why not, for gosh sake!
That's the only way we can help him."

"It might not be helpin' him," remarked Hashknife. "Can't yuh see what happened, Lank? The
man I shot through the door last night is in bad
shape. They kidnapped Doc and his wife, after
makin' Doc fix the feller up. Maybe Doc knows
who they are. They took Doc and his wife along—
and they only let Doc come back. If Doc opens
his mouth about it, they'll kill his wife. Don'tcha
see why he wouldn't dare talk anything about
it?"

"Yea-a-a-ah!" breathed Lank. "Yuh know, I figured that somethin' like that—"

"Be honest about it," said Honey.

"All right," sighed Lank. "I'll admit that there

are angles that I didn't figure out. But what are we goin' to do, Hashknife?"

Hashknife ignored the question for one of his own.

"Lank, how far does the railroad run along the rim of this valley?" he asked.

"Oh, about fifteen miles, I reckon, before it swings through the Twin Sisters Pass."

"Are there any mines along that railroad—along the rim?"

"No operatin' mines, Hashknife. There's the Old Mission mine, but it closed a year ago."

"I see. Did they had a spur track up there?"

"They had a sidetrack where they used to load. I suppose it's still there. But what is this all about?"

"I don't know yet, Lank. Does anybody know if Ed Jones went back to the rim?"

"I don't think so," said Honey. "He went out to the Circle H, and I don't know if he's still there, or not. Franz said he'd have to hire another man to work with him, after Dobbs, or Adams, was cut out of the pack."

"If he comes to town, let me know," said Hashknife. "I'd kinda like to get a look at the gent—as long as he came here with Curt Adams."

After Hashknife and Sleepy left the office, Lank remarked, "Yuh know, it's kinda funny."

"What is?" queried Honey.

"This Hartley person, actin' like he was takin' over this whole deal, askin' questions and all that stuff. After all, I'm the sheriff—and this is my job. I don't exactly like it. Oh, I know—I've heard

57

you lie about what he's done; so yuh don't have to start all over again."

"I'm glad yo're satisfied that he's the man to take over the deal," said Honey. "I'd hate to have to convince yuh. My head hurts too much for arguments."

Lank stepped over and picked up his hat, jerking it down tightly on his head. He walked to the doorway and turned his head to remark:

"I can't blame it on that crack yuh got last night, 'cause you didn't have any sense before that."

"No, I don't reckon I did," admitted Honey soberly, "but my ignorant thoughts were better connected, don't yuh think, Lank?"

CHAPTER 7

Hashknife and Sleepy were in front of the hotel when four men rode in and tied up at the War Eagle Saloon. They recognized three of them as Nick Enright, Jud Gibson and Tobe Hansen, owners of the Circle H—but the fourth man was a stranger.

"Could be Ed Jones, their rim-rider," remarked Sleepy.

After the four men entered the saloon, Hashknife and Sleepy went over there. The four were at the bar, and Enright spoke to Hashknife, calling him by name. The stranger, a slattern-looking cowpoke, with a long nose and small eyes, looked Hashknife over critically, then said to Enright:

"Hartley, eh? So this is the feller who made me a rim-widder, eh?"

Hashknife stopped and looked sharply at Ed

Jones, who became a bit confused and apologetic.

"I—I wasn't tryin' to be smart, Mister," he said. "Dobbs didn't mean a thing to me. I jist meant that you made me go it alone."

"I've been tellin' Ed that he's better off alone," said Enright quickly.

"What's all the fuss about?" asked Hashknife calmly. "After all, Mr. Dobbs, alias Curt Adams, made the first move."

"Shore, shore!" agreed Jones heartily. "No hard feelin's."

"None," said Hashknife. "Everythin' is fine with me."

Jud Gibson spun his empty glass across the bar and said, "Ed, you might as well get yore grub and head for the rim. I'll ask Clint Franz to send a man up there as soon as he can."

"All right," nodded Jones, and finished his drink.

Back at the hotel, Hashknife admitted that he didn't recognize Ed Jones. Honey Moon came up and sat down with them.

"I had a bright idea, Hashknife," he said. "Some worthy citizen of Piute Valley is nursin' a bullet hole, and I figured that all we'd have to do is find out who he is. Doc won't talk. Lank figured out that by the time we'd checked up on everybody in the valley—well, the man would either be well or dead a long time."

Clint Franz came to town that afternoon. Hashknife and Sleepy met him in front of the general store. Franz looked old and drawn today. He said he had received a telegram from the sheriff at Red Bank, saying that they had found no trace of his son.

"They're offerin' a thousand dollars reward for Rowdy," he said wearily, "so I'm goin' to boost it another thousand."

"That's fine," said Hashknife, "if you'll offer that extra thousand for him, alive and well."

"What do you mean, Hartley?" asked Franz curiously.

"I mean that I don't want murder to show a profit."

"Profit?"

"Yes—profit. I've known a lot of men who will kill yuh for a lot less than that. Suppose somebody knows exactly where Rowdy is—and they want blood money, before they'll act."

Clint Franz stared at Hashknife thoughtfully. "You mean—Rowdy didn't get away?" he said.

"I hope he did—he'd be safer. Have you sent another man to the rim?"

"No, I haven't been able to find a man to—well, the average cowpoke don't like that sort of a job. It's lonesome."

"Franz, just where would yore man be located up there? Is it near the Old Mission mine?"

Franz looked sharply at Hashknife, wondering at the question.

"Why, yeah, they're camped right near there. But what—"

"Have you got a man yuh can trust? I mean, a man who can't be bought; a man who won't hesitate to shoot."

"Hartley, what is this all about?"

"It's about sheep, my friend. I wouldn't trust Ed Jones as far as I could drop-kick a steer. Suppose some night, along about the twentieth of this month, a trainload of sheep pulled into the sidin' at the mine—and unloaded. Before you fellows could do a thing about it, there'd be sheep all over the back ranges."

"That's true, Hartley; we've realized it for a long time."

"And in spite of that, you've hired an escaped murderer and another man I wouldn't trust, to guard the most vital spot on the rim."

"I won't argue with yuh on that. Of course, I didn't know that Dobbs was a bad man."

"And you also didn't *know* he was a good man, Franz."

"You spoke about the twentieth. If you've got any evidence of the sheepmen—we'll call a meetin' of the cattlemen right away."

"And that," declared Hanshknife, "would be just about as sensible as yore quarrel with Luke Neves."

Clint Franz's jaw sagged for a moment, his eyes blinking fast.

"Just what did yuh mean by that remark, Hartley?" he asked.

"I mean that somebody in this valley has made a fool out of both of yuh, Franz. Think it over."

Clint Franz was inclined to get angry, but wasn't quite sure just what Hashknife meant. He said, "What am I supposed to think over?"

"All the things that have happened since that phony buyer came here to start trouble between you and the Forty-Four."

"Phony buyer, eh?"

"Yeah—a smart troublemaker. Think it over, Franz."

They went into the store, leaving Clint Franz on the edge of the sidewalk, scowling thoughtfully under the brim of his sombrero. After a few moments he went back to his horse and rode down to the sheriff's office.

About a half hour later Honey Moon came up to the hotel. The fat deputy didn't look too happy, as he sat down and began rolling a smoke with his pudgy fingers.

"Somethin' on yore mind?" asked Sleepy.

"What I've got left of it," replied Honey. "Lank's kinda on the warpath, and he takes it out on me."

"What's itchin' him now?" asked Hashknife.

"You."

"Me?"

Honey sighed and leaned back, nodding his head.

"Lank's all right," he said slowly, "but he's got a jealous streak. Seems like he got himself irked over you. He seems to kinda feel that you're a lot smarter than he is, and if there's anythin' that Lank hates, it's smart folks. Sometimes he jumps on me."

"I can imagine that," said Sleepy dryly.

"The fact of the matter is," stated Honey, "he sent me here to tell yuh that from now on, he'll handle the case."

"What case?" asked Hashknife curiously.

"Well, he didn't jist specify, Hashknife. I think he means the case of Doc Willis. Don't ask me how he'll handle it. I saw Doc a while ago, and he's lower than a snake's belly. Won't talk, won't eat—and he never did drink. It's shore a good thing that Luke Neves is out of danger, 'cause Doc wouldn't know a snakebite from a case of measles."

"Just how is Lank goin' to handle the case?" asked Hashknife.

"Wrong, of course—but that's his job. He don't even want my help."

"Maybe Doc has told him somethin'," suggested Sleepy.

"Nope. All Doc does is nod or shake—mostly shake. Franz was down at the office a while ago, talkin' with Lank. I didn't hear what they was talkin' about, but I did hear yore name mentioned, and it wasn't with any great reverence, I'll say that. It was somethin' about a meetin' of the cattlemen."

"That's interestin'," remarked Hashknife.

"You'll respect his wishes?" asked Honey.

"Yeah, I'll do that," replied Hashknife. "After all, it's none of my business."

"That's exactly what Lank said, and he added the word damn."

Honey went back to report to Lank Morris. Sleepy was indignant.

"None of our damn business, eh? How do yuh like that, pardner?"

"All right," smiled Hashknife. "After all, he's right. If I was the sheriff, I'd hate to have a stranger come in and run things."

"That's right," agreed Sleepy. "It ain't ethical, as yuh might say. How about me and you pilin' on our broncs and headin' for a fresh hill? We ain't welcome—not by Lank Morris."

Hashknife looked thoughtfully at Sleepy, a thin smile on his lips, as he said, "If there was only Lank Morris to consider—yeah, we'd pull out."

"Well, if he don't want us—"

"I'm thinkin' about a man who is shy a son—and Doc Willis—shy a wife—and a man who warned us to pray or run, Sleepy."

"Yeah, that's right. I forgot about them."

Sleepy relaxed and began rolling a cigarette.

They saw Honey after supper that evening, but he got away from them as quickly as possible. Doctor Willis' horse and buggy was tied to his front fence, indicating that he might be going to make a call that night. Hashknife looked it over soberly. There was something decidedly wrong about the whole layout, in his mind, at least.

As soon as it was dark, Hashknife and Sleepy left the hotel from the rear, circled far around the town and came in behind the doctor's home, where they found a fairly comfortable place to stretch out on the ground in some low brush.

"If it was me," declared Sleepy, "I'd watch that horse and buggy."

"Lank's prob'ly doin' that right now," said Hashknife.

"And what are we doin' out here?" asked Sleepy.

Hashknife laughed quietly. "Makin' fools of ourselves, I reckon—unless my hunch works out."

For two hours they remained quiet, wishing for a smoke, but not daring to light a match. They

65

could see a dim light in one of Doc Willis' windows at the rear of the house, but not a sound. They were unable to see if the horse and buggy were still there. Suddenly Hashknife touched Sleepy on the arm. Behind them and to their left was a man, crawling on his hands and knees. He went past them, and disappeared somewhere vaguely around the rear of the house.

"Stay right here," whispered Hashknife, and began heading back the way the man had come.

It didn't require a lot of searching for Hashknife to find two saddled horses near an old shed. Quickly he lighted a match, shielding it closely, and examined both horses and riding-rigs. As he started back he heard men walking, and quickly dropped into the weeds. At the horses he heard a voice say:

"All right, Doc—get on."

In a few moments they were riding away from the house, and disappeared in the darkness.

Lank Morris and Honey Moon, hidden across the street from the doctor's place, saw the doctor leave the house, go quietly to the buggy and drive away. Their horses were hidden behind an old tight-board fence, and in a few moments they were following the buggy.

"They can't fool me," declared Lank. "I don't need any help. We can find out where Doc's goin'—and nab the gang."

An hour later, far out on an old deserted road, they found the horse and buggy, the horse tied to a tree, but no sign of the doctor. Honey said, "Good gosh, Lank! Nobody lives out around here. This old road don't run more'n a mile further."

They went in carefully, lighted a match and examined the buggy seat. Here was a soiled sheet of paper, on which was printed in smudged pencil:

SHERIF PLEZE RETURN RIG TO DOCS PLACE.

The match burned to Lank's fingers and he threw it away with a bitter bit of profanity.

"It don't look like a gang nab to me, Lank," announced Honey.

"All right, don't get smart," growled the sheriff. "Get in that buggy and drive it back—I'll lead yore horse."

Of course, the buggy and horse were gone from Doctor Willis' fence when Hashknife and Sleepy went back to the hotel. There was no sign of Lank Morris nor Honey Moon. As they undressed in their room, Sleepy said:

"Didja find out anythin', Hashknife?"

"Well, I'm not sure—yet; but I know more than I did, pardner."

Lank Morris was very unhappy over everything. When they left the horse and buggy in front of the doctor's home, he said to Honey, "If you open yore mouth about this deal, I'll get me a new deputy."

Honey Moon, stiff and disgruntled, replied: "Yeah, and if you don't start showin' some brains, they'll be hirin' a new sheriff, too. You may not want any help, but you can't prove from that that yuh don't need some."

CHAPTER 8

THE NEXT MORNING LANK MORRIS GOT A TELEGRAM from Brass Hinkley at Echo Pass, which said:

FOR YOUR OWN INFORMATION ROWDY FRANZ IS ON HIS WAY HOME FROM HERE.

Lank pocketed the telegram, and didn't even tell Honey about it. Honey wanted to tell Hashknife and Sleepy what happened to him and the sheriff, but Lank kept him busy around the office. He wanted Honey there when Rowdy Franz showed up, but Rowdy didn't show up.

Honey was sweeping out the jail, when Clint Franz and three of his men rode in and stopped at the office. Honey, working in the short corridor, leaned on his old broom and listened, unseen, to what Clint Franz had to say—and it was plenty.

"All right," said Clint, "just keep yore shirt on, Lank. Rowdy has been held prisoner in an old shack about three miles from Echo Pass, but he slipped his ropes and got away. He's at the ranch, tryin' to get enough to eat."

"All right," said Lank Morris. "Keep talkin', Clint."

"I'll do that. Rowdy didn't know Luke Neves was shot. When Rowdy went to get the horses, somebody knocked him out. They kept him blindfolded, but they didn't plug his ears, and he heard plenty. Hartley and Stevens are workin' for the sheep interests, and they're in here to hoodwink all of us."

"No!" exclaimed the astonished sheriff.

"Yes!" rasped Clint Franz. "Rowdy couldn't hear all of it, but those fools laughed and talked about what suckers Hartley and Stevens were makin' of Piute Valley. And they have, I believe."

"Not as much as you may think," replied the sheriff grimly. "I haven't trusted 'em as much as they think. Playin' me for a fool, eh? But how did Rowdy get loose?"

"Squawked about 'em ropin' him so tight that it was killin' him, and they gave him enough slack to get loose. Had his horse in an old shed— and Rowdy lit a shuck out of there."

"Well, what's to be done?" asked one of the men.

"We can't arrest 'em," said the sheriff. "After all, they ain't busted any laws."

"We can give 'em a ten-count to git out of the valley."

"Wait a minute," said Lank. "If we run 'em out of the valley, we'll never know what the scheme was. My idea is to give 'em enough rope to hang themselves. We'll watch 'em every minute. In that way, maybe we can find out what this is all about."

"Rowdy says that Hartley and Stevens are big guns in the sheep outfit. He says he heard that it was the sheep outfit that killed Dell Meek, 'cause he had found out how they was goin' to put the woolies into Piute Valley."

Lank Morris drew a deep breath of satisfaction and said:

"Boys, that calls for a drink. Let's go over and have it."

They trooped out and went across the street. Honey Moon came into the office, dragging his broom, and stood in the doorway. It was rather difficult for Honey to look grim, but he was giving his own particular version of a grim expression.

Honey wanted to be honest with Lank Morris, and he also wanted to be honest with his own conscience. Finally he took a sheet of paper, crudely printed a single line on it with a pen, pinned his badge to it, and placed it back on the desk. The line read:

I CAN'T KEEP MY DAMN MOUTH SHUT.

HONEY.

70

Then he walked out, closed the office door, and headed for the hotel.

Hashknife and Sleepy sat in their room, listening calmly to Honey's recital of what was said in the office. Honey was just a little disappointed at their attitude.

"Good gosh, I quit my job to tell yuh this—and you don't even snort over the news," he grunted.

"You mean—you resigned?" asked Sleepy.

"I shore did. I wrote m' resignation, pinned my badge onto it and walked out."

"You get back there and grab that letter!" ordered Hashknife. "Yo're worth more to us in office than out. Make it fast!"

But Honey was too late. Lank had just seated himself at the desk, and was looking at the resignation as Honey came through from the jail. Lank got to his feet, flung the badge on the desk-top and said harshly:

"So you sold out to the sheep, too, eh?"

Honey's first punch missed Lank's jaw by exactly three feet, because Honey forgot that the desk was between them, but that did not daunt the angry deputy, who didn't miss the next one. The battle between the short, fat deputy, and the long, lean sheriff should have been one-sided. Lank dodged blows very well, but left his middle exposed, and when the fight was over, Honey went up the street, decidedly unsteady on both bow-legs, and sporting a badly discolored left eye, while Lank Morris reposed serenely behind his own desk, one leg up over the chair, and wondering dimly if he would ever get enough wind in his lungs to support them.

71

Clint Franz and his men went over from the saloon to have one last word with Lank Morris before going back to the ranch, and they found Lank leaning against his desk, much the worse for wear. There was a busted chair in the middle of the office, and everything, except the desk, was in terrible disorder.

"What on earth happened?" asked Franz.

"Huh-Honey resigned," wheezed Lank.

"He shore resigns awful hard," remarked a cowboy dryly.

"What caused the trouble?" asked Franz curiously.

"I—I'll be all right—pretty soon," whispered the sheriff. "I guess I didn't keep my damn mouth shut."

"All right, Lank—we're headin' home, and I'm sendin' word to all the cowmen to meet here tonight. We've got to meet this issue squarely. I'll put yore scheme up to them. If they want to wait—all right, but my idea is to run them two spies out of the valley—and I don't mean with kid gloves."

"I'll go along with any scheme you've got," said Lank miserably, "but I don't think that runnin' 'em out will solve it."

After the Lazy F crew pulled out, Mrs. Neves and Laura came in a buggy. Mrs. Neves said, "Something has to be done, sheriff. Doctor Willis was gone all night, and came back on foot, so tired that he couldn't do anything. My husband must have attention."

"Yes'm," admitted the harassed sheriff wearily. "I don't know what to do. I've been so busy—"

"Doing what?" asked Mrs. Neves.

"Will yuh please go home and let me alone?" he pleaded. "I'm doin' everything I can. Doc won't tell where he goes—nor when—nor what he does when he gets there. Yore husband ain't in no danger now—Doc said so. I—I've got things to do."

"Where is Mr. Hartley?" asked Laura.

"Mr. Hartley? Why, I—I suppose he's plannin' just how to sheep out Piute Valley."

"What do you mean?" demanded the girl in astonishment.

"Hartley and his partner are sheep spies, if you must know. You can tell that to yore father—and the crew. I'm sick and tired of the whole thing. Everybody blames me. I—I wish—"

"What do you wish?" asked Laura, ready to laugh.

"I wish folks would let me alone for a while. I've got to think a lot and I can't, with everybody botherin' me."

"Where is Honey?" asked Laura.

"I don't know and I don't care. He quit me this afternoon."

"You don't mean that Honey quit his job," said Mrs. Neves.

Lank winced from the pain of a sore rib, but nodded slowly.

"He must have been fooling," said Laura.

"If he was," sighed Lank, "I'd hate to meet him when he happened to be in dead earnest."

* * *

He stood in the doorway and watched them drive away. As he shifted his tired eyes around, here was Hashknife Hartley, coming down toward the office. Lank groaned and went inside, sat down at his desk and picked up a half-smoked cigar. Hashknife came in, just as though nothing had happened, and sat down.

"What's new, Lank?" he asked casually, as he began rolling a cigarette. Lank didn't say, he merely watched those long fingers shape the cigarette.

"By the way, Lank, have you got a brand register here?" asked his caller.

The sheriff took the register from a desk drawer and shoved it across the desk.

"Thank yuh," said Hashknife. "I just wanted to check up on somethin'! How's Doc comin' with his problem?"

"I suppose Honey told yuh what happened last night."

Hashknife didn't look up, as he replied, "Yeah, he did."

"Hartley, if yuh're interested—you ain't wanted here."

"That's good," replied Hashknife, concentrating on a certain brand. "I'd hate to be wanted by the law."

"I didn't mean the law, Hartley."

"Oh, I see. Well," Hashknife handed the book back and inhaled deeply on his cigarette, "yuh can't make everybody like yuh. It just ain't human nature, Lank. Oh, I know—they're sayin' we're sheep spies. Not very complimentary, my

74

friend. If I was in charge of things like that, I'd have had sheep in here months ago."

"Yuh think so, eh?"

"Sure. Knot-heads, fightin' each other, sendin' anybody to guard the rim. Lank, I'm surprised there's any cattle range left, 'cause cowmen are so dumb. And you, my friend, have trailed right along with them. Well, I'll see yuh later."

"Wait a minute!" snapped Lank, as Hashknife reached the doorway. "If you will take my advice, you'll both pull out now. Tonight the cattlemen are meetin' here in the courthouse—to decide what to do with you and your sneakin' pardner."

Hashknife looked at Lank, a wide grin on his face.

"Thank yuh, Lank," he said pleasantly. "Now that I know—maybe I can save a few skins—includin' our own."

Lank Morris stared at the empty doorway, got to his feet and went over there, looking up the street, where Hashknife was walking slowly along the sidewalk.

"Now, what in the devil did he mean by that?" asked Lank aloud. "Save skins? So we're all dumb, eh? And when I told him—he never turned a hair. I'll say he's got nerve—the frozen kind."

Hashknife crossed the street to the War Eagle Saloon, but stopped at the hitchrack, where he looked at a gray horse closely, after which he sauntered back into the hotel.

After thinking it over, Lank went down to Doctor Willis' place, where he found Laura, acting as nurse and cook. The doctor was asleep on a couch, and Laura told Lank that he still would not talk about what had happened to Mrs. Willis. Lank told them what Clint Franz told him—that Rowdy was home again, unhurt, and that he had nothing to do with the shooting of Luke Neves.

Laura almost hugged Lank for the news, but Luke Neves was neither joyous nor convinced. He said, "Rowdy could tell anythin'. It still don't prove he didn't do it."

Laura said, "Until it is proved, I don't believe Mr. Hartley and Mr. Stevens are crooks."

Lank didn't try to convince them—he let it drop. After all, he knew that arguments never worked out right for him; so he went back, dropped in at the livery stable and told the stableman to let him know the minute Hartley or Stevens took their horses.

From the window at the hotel, Sleepy saw Lank go to the stable, and told the others. Hashknife merely smiled, as he remarked:

"Lank's gettin' nervous. I'll bet he's all set to know just when we ride away—if we do."

"Are we?" asked Honey Moon.

"Keep holdin' that raw beef on yore eye and don't ask questions," advised Sleepy. "After all, yuh might need two eyes."

CHAPTER 9

JUST BEFORE DARK THEY WENT TO THE STABLE AND saddled their horses, and rode swiftly out of town, circled back and tied up at an old shed behind the hotel. Honey was curious as to why Hashknife wanted to do this, and Hashknife explained that he didn't want the sheriff trailing them. They were back in their room, before the stableman was able to find Lank Morris and tell him. They watched Lank ride away swiftly, taking the same direction out of town.

A short time later they went back to their horses and Hashknife asked Honey if he knew of a way they could go to the Circle H and not chance meeting anyone on the road. Honey did.

"But why go out to the Circle H?" asked Honey. "After all—"

"Honey," explained Hashknife indulgently, "this is just another of my crazy ideas."

"Oh, well, shore—we'll see if it works."

Honey took them in a roundabout way, but brought them back on the road about a mile from the Circle H, where they found Lank's horse, loose, one bridle-rein broken at the bit. They examined the horse and riding rig as well as they could in the dark, and tied the animal beside the road.

"Somethin' has happened to Lank," declared Honey, "and I wonder what it is."

"Prob'ly fell off his horse," said Sleepy, "and walked back."

"Could be," agreed Honey. "I shore worked him over somethin' wonderful today."

"Stop braggin' and lead us around the ranch house, where we won't be seen," advised Sleepy.

They came in through a thicket of willows and pulled up behind the old swaybacked stable. Walking quietly they crawled through a fence and came in close to the stable, where they could hide behind an old pile of lumber and a broken-down wagon. There was a light in the ranch house, but the windows were covered.

"Get comfortable," whispered Hashknife, " 'cause we may be here for quite a while."

"Are we lookin' for anythin' in particular?" asked Honey.

"No-o-o, just a general inspection," replied Hashknife. "Maybe my idea is no good—but it's the only one I've got; so we'll try it out."

They had been there about an hour, when three riders came in and tied up at the corral fence. They went into the house. Nothing happened for another hour, when a man left the house, came to the stable, where they heard him saddling a horse, and in a few minutes he rode away, heading for War Eagle.

"I reckon that was Jud Gibson, headin' for that meetin' in town," Honey whispered.

"He's their head man, eh?" queried Hashknife.

"He reps for the Circle H," replied Honey. "Hashknife, you don't figure that the Circle H are a bad bunch, do yuh?"

"What do you think about 'em, Honey?"

"Why, they're a good bunch of fellers."

"That's fine. Honey, who owns the sheep north of here?"

"Riggs Caldwell owns the most of 'em. He's sort of a sheep king, I reckon."

Another hour passed without any action from the house. Honey was getting tired of sprawling on the ground, but Sleepy said, "You ain't got no more bones than we have, feller—and you've got a blamed sight more upholstery."

Suddenly there were three more horses coming in, pulling up at the house, where two people went into the house, and the third one took the horses down to the corral fence. They saw him go back to the house, and Honey whispered excitedly:

"One of them was a woman, Hashknife!"

"Yeah, I think so. I don't figure that sort of thing."

Hashknife slid to his feet, hunched behind the old wagon, as he whispered, "You two stay here; I'm goin' prospectin'. If anythin' busts up there, come runnin'."

Then he was gone, circling the corral and along the willows.

"If anythin' busts?" queried Honey. "What might bust?"

"I don't know, Honey—but when Hashknife says things might bust—they usually do. Take it easy, will yuh?"

Hashknife, traveling with all the stealth of a marauding Apache, circled the rear of the house, and came in on the opposite side. The windows on that side were all dark, and he was unable to hear any voices. Sliding along, all senses alert, he came to what seemed to be the outside, slanting doors of a cellar. Feeling carefully he found that the doors were unlocked, the padlock open and hanging on a staple.

Slowly he opened half of the door, resting it easily against some bushes. Through the doorway he could hear voices. Slipping quietly down the dirt steps, he lowered the door behind him. There were cracks in the old flooring, and he could hear sounds quite plain, and also see a little light through the cracks. The cellar proved to be about five feet deep, eight feet long and about five feet wide. There was a short ladder, nailed to one side of what seemed to be a trapdoor.

Suddenly there was a rattling sound at the outside door, and a voice said, "Yeah, yuh better lock it—it'd be safer."

Hashknife heard them snap the padlock, and walk away. Quickly he went back to the door. There was a wide crack between the two doors and his exploring fingers were able to prove that the padlock had been closed, locking him very securely in the cellar.

Hashknife moved back to the far end, where a floor crack gave him a chance to hear what was being said by a querulous voice.

"Yes, I know all about Hartley gettin' wise to the date. But we've had that changed, and tonight, at midnight, that first trainload will head for the spur-track at the Mission mine. By daylight we'll be unloadin'. Ed Jones is handlin' that part of the rim alone so our big problem is over—unless your crazy actions tonight bring the whole thing down on our heads."

"We couldn't help it," complained a voice. "You said we'd have to finish the doctor tonight, but he wasn't there. That damn female wouldn't talk, so we tried to make her, and she tore my mask off. What could we do in a case like that—walk out—with her knowin' who I am? As far as me bein' wrong, what about you grabbin' the sheriff?"

"He walked in on us—we couldn't do anythin' else. Here I am, almost ready to ride again—and what happens? Oh, I'll ride—if it kills me. After tonight, we can't be here any longer."

"That's sensible," remarked another voice. "But what's ahead of us—dodgin' the law for the rest of our lives?"

"Listen!" snapped one of the men. "A rider just came!"

There was a babel of muffled voices, the closing of a door, and a man saying, "Hartley, Stevens and Moon pulled out just at dark, and Lank Morris followed—uh—so yuh got 'em, eh? Good!"

"We got Morris—not the others. Did they come this way?"

"How do I know? If Morris trailed 'em—"

The querulous voice broke in sharply:

"Stop talkin', will yuh? Take the three of 'em, see that they're well tied and dump 'em in the cellar. As soon as Gib comes back from the meetin', and we know what's bein' done, we'll load 'em on horses and take 'em to the HEH. Nobody would ever think of lookin' for 'em up there."

"Wait a minute!" snapped a new voice. "Doc played square, and the old lady saved yore life. Why not play square and send her home? She's a nice old lady, and she's deservin' of a break."

"And shove our necks into a noose? Yo're a bigger fool than yuh look."

"She goes home, I tell yuh. I've got a mother and—no, you don't!"

A gun blasted and a man cried out sharply. For several moments there was not a word. Then the querulous voice announced:

"I'm runnin' this deal—yet—and don't forget it. See that they're all tied up good, and dump 'em into the cellar."

"Why not put 'em on horses now and pull out?"

"Not until Gib gets here; we've got to know what was done."

Hashknife heard them move the table from over the trapdoor, and squeezed himself against the wall behind the ladder. It was a tight fit, and shielded him from those above. He was in a very precarious position just now. They lifted the trapdoor, and one man came down, almost brushing against Hashknife. Quickly they slid three bound figures over the edge of the trap, and the man, panting from the effort, stacked them in the narrow space. All three of them were gagged.

As the man turned from his last deposit and came back to the ladder, hunched over, Hashknife swung his six-shooter in a short arc, and the intruder went down without a sound. The others were moving back into the living room, as Hashknife, covered with dirt and cobwebs, came up the ladder, and got quickly to his feet.

It was only three steps to the entrance to the main room, and as he stepped into the lamplight, Enright screamed:

"Hartley! Look out!"

Hashknife's gun blasted from his hip, and Enright went into the wall, doing a improvised tapdance. There were three more men in the room, in sight, and Hashknife realized that the odds were just a bit heavy, as bullets splintered the casing of the door, spraying him with pieces of wood. He stepped back quickly, felt himself going into space, and came down heavily in the cellar, the unconscious outlaw breaking his fall.

Dazed for the moment, he realized that they had slammed the trapdoor shut over him. He rolled over, clawed for the outside door and managed to grasp the padlock. Holding it with his left hand, he shoved the muzzle of his forty-five against it, and pulled the trigger. It numbed his left hand for the moment, but the hasp and padlock went flying.

He banged his shoulders against the two doors, flinging them wide open, and went lunging into the open. He heard shots fired on the other side of the house as he went running in that direction. He heard Sleepy yelling:

"How much lead does it take to load yuh down?"

Hashknife went running down to the corral fence, calling for Sleepy. One man was down, two more had their hands high, as Honey danced around, begging them to fight it out.

"Are yuh all right?" asked Sleepy anxiously.

"Fine as frawg-hair," panted Hashknife. "You've got three? That must leave one more in there. Good work! Tie 'em tight, boys; we need some survivors."

There were plenty ropes on the saddles, and the two men were quickly tied. There was a little moonlight now. A man was going toward the rickety porch, hunched over, limping.

"Who on earth is that? He's got a rifle or a shotgun?" said Sleepy.

Slowly they moved in behind him, having no idea who it might be. The stranger paid no attention to them, as he limped ahead. Coming into the illumination of the lamp in the main room, he stepped into the open doorway, the gun lifted to his shoulder. A man screamed:

"No, no! Don't do that! I'll—"

But the heavy shotgun blasted once—twice. It kicked the man around and he sat down on the step, facing Hashknife, Sleepy and Honey Moon.

He was Doctor Willis, too tired to care what happened. The gun slipped from his fingers and banged on the porch.

"Nice work, Doc," said Hashknife.

The old practitioner looked up at him, staring, his lips moving.

"Yes, I believe so," he said, and keeled over in a faint.

"My God!" gasped Sleepy. "I'll bet he walked all the way out here!"

"I'll bet it was worth it—to him. C'mon."

Hansen was dead, Enright badly hurt, but able to curse. Down in the cellar were Laura Neves, Mrs. Willis and Lank Morris, none the worse for wear, but without any understanding of what had happened.

On a cot was Bob Cole, supposed to be owner of the HEH ranch near Echo Pass, loaded with buckshot.

Lank Morris said, "Honey, what happened? Why, I—say somethin', can't yuh?"

"I don't know what happened, blast it! Nobody does—except Hashknife. I—I just came along—for the ride."

Hashknife pulled out his old watch and glanced at it. Then he turned and looked at Doc Willis and his wife, sitting there, looking at each other, as though both had discovered something entirely new in life.

"Sleepy," said Hashknife, "you take over here; me and Lank have got to hit the grit—and the time is short. See yuh later. C'mon, Lank."

They didn't wait to select horses—they took the nearest ones, and went galloping back toward War Eagle. Lank didn't ask questions, but followed Hashknife's lead. They swept into town and pulled up at the courthouse, where at least two dozen horses were tied to a low fence.

"Where's the meetin', Lank?" asked Hash-knife. "You lead the way."

They went running up the steps and down a corridor. They could hear voices raised in argument, and one said:

"I make a motion that we escort 'em out of the valley. And if they put up a battle—start shootin'. Those two men are enemies of Piute Valley and of all decent cowmen."

Hashknife flung the door open, and they went inside. At least two dozen men were in that smoke-fogged room and Jud Gibson was on the platform, making his motion. Every man in the room jerked around as the door banged shut behind Hashknife and Lank. Gibson's hand dropped to his side and he stepped back.

"There's one of 'em!" he yelled. "Of all the nerve!"

Hashknife walked slowly down the aisle, paying no attention to the others, his eyes centered on Jud Gibson. At the edge of the platform, he stopped short, looking at Gibson.

At a table on the platform sat Clint Franz, and beside him sat Rowdy Franz. Rowdy had been Exhibit A in this meeting. No one spoke. The crowd sensed drama, leaning forward, waiting for it to happen. Then Hashknife spoke, slowly and distinctly:

"Mr. Franz, have you a paper and pencil on the table?"

"Yes, I—what is this all about, Hartley?"

But Hashknife ignored the question. "Gibson, go over to that table," he said. "I'm sure Mr. Franz will let yuh have his chair. And do it now!"

Gibson's fingers flexed, his eyes hard, as he

looked at Hashknife. Then he said, "Am I to let this sheep spy give orders here?"

"You better do it, Gibson—and do it now!"

Slowly Gibson went over to the table, his eyes on Hashknife. Franz got to his feet and Gibson sat down. Most of the blood had drained from Gibson's face, and his fingers shook as he picked up the pencil. Hashknife said, "You better let Franz write it, Gibson—yore nerve is all in yore fingers."

Franz took the pencil, and Hashknife began slowly:

"It is now ten minutes after eleven, gentlemen. Franz, this is a telegram, sent to Riggs Caldwell. I believe he's at Maricopa. And here is what to write, Franz:

" 'Cole and Hansen are dead. Enright and two of your men are crippled, the others in jail. Don't attempt to ship sheep here.'

"And," added Hashknife, "you can sign Gibson's name."

It was too much for Gibson. He went out of that chair as though he had a coiled spring under him, landed almost against a window, whirled with a gun in his hand, but at that moment Hashknife blasted, and Gibson's gun went flying when the bullet broke his right arm. Gibson went down against the wall, cursing bitterly.

"Don't wait to ask questions, Franz!" snapped Hashknife. "Get that telegram on the wire—they ship sheep to Piute Valley at midnight!"

"I'll take it!" gasped Rowdy. "At least, I can do that right," and went running from the room.

"I'll talk," said Lank Morris. "They had me prisoner at the Circle H—me and Mrs. Willis and

Laura Neves. Hartley broke up the gang—I don't now how. Damn it, this was a nightmare! I heard their plots. Bob Cole, owner of the HEH outfit was the man Hartley shot through the door. They forced Doc Willis to attend him, and they had Mrs. Willis. They'd have killed her, if he told. The sheep interests own the HEH and the Circle H. I don't know how Hartley found out—but he did. They killed Dell Meek 'cause he knew they were sheepmen. Enright shot Luke Neves, tryin' to prevent Laura from marryin' Rowdy, by cinchin' him for the job. Oh, they talked about things. Maybe I wasn't to came out alive. And they talked about Hashknife and Sleepy, bein' sheep spies, before they let Rowdy loose to come here and tell it. I tell yuh, they were smart."

"They made a mistake," said Hashknife quietly, "a mistake that you men should have figured out. They wanted to control both the Lazy F and the Forty-Four; so they started a war, while they also rustled cows, took 'em in the Echo Pass country, and rebranded 'em. Yuh see, gents—you can take a Lazy F or a Forty-Four and make it into an HEH, connected brand, as easy as drawin' straight lines. I'm very sure that Riggs Caldwell had nothin' to do with the stealin' and sellin' of yore cattle."

Franz turned to Gibson and asked, "Can you add anythin' to that, Gib?"

"Only," said Gibson, through set teeth, "we should have killed him the day he showed up at Echo Pass."

"Thank yuh," said Hashknife simply, and walked out.

CHAPTER 10

IT WAS ABOUT TWO HOURS LATER, WITH EVERYTHING fixed up, and with most everybody in War Eagle, it seemed, grouped in the lobby of the hotel. Rowdy and Laura were there, Clint Franz, Mrs. Neves, Doc Willis and his wife, Honey Moon, proud of his black eye, and once more deputy sheriff, after urging by Lank Morris.

Oscar Odom said apologetically:

"I know exactly how you folks feel. Sort of a day of deliverance, and all that, but—well, them two boys have gone to bed. They said they was all fagged out, and—well, I'd hate to wake 'em up."

"I'll go with you, Oscar," piped the doctor. "I'm sure they will understand, and not object to—shall we go up, Oscar?"

The crowd waited, but only the two old-timers

came back. Oscar Odom placed a five-dollar bill on the desk and faced the crowd.

"I found that money, coverin' their bill, on the bed," he said. "That's all, folks—they're gone. I dunno—where."

Far out on a lonely road in the hills, riding knee-to-knee in the moonlight, were the two "wanted" men. Ahead was the jagged outlines of tall hills, sharp against the stars.

"They'd prob'ly have a crowd back there in War Eagle," remarked Sleepy.

"Yeah," sighed Hashknife, "I reckon so, pardner."

"Maybe wantin' to take up a collection to build a monument, or offerin' to pay us for doin' the job, figurin' we needed pay, I suppose."

"Biggest payment I ever got," said Hashknife quietly.

"What do yuh mean—biggest payment?"

"When the ruckus was over at the Circle H, pardner; did you see Doc and his wife, lookin' at each other? That was my payoff."

And they went along, with only the jingle of bit-chains and the clicking of hoofs—heading for another hill.

THE REDHEAD
OF AZTEC WELLS

CHAPTER 1
Tragedy on the AA

JOHNNY AVERY WAS A VERY DISCOURAGED YOUNG cowboy. In fact, Johnny was only twelve years of age, minus a horse and saddle, his feet so badly blistered, cut and bruised that he could hardly walk, and he was still miles from home. He sat on a rock on the edge of Ghost Canyon, a disconsolate-looking youngster, his boots beside him.

Johnny was red-headed, freckled, his eyes as blue as the sky over the canyon, but sad now. Johnny had traveled about twenty-five miles from home, looking for two strayed horses. That part was not so unusual, but a bank along a deep washout had broken down, letting Johnny and his horse fall about thirty feet, with the result that the horse suffered a broken neck. Johnny was badly bruised, but unbroken.

This had happened yesterday. Since then Johnny had walked miles, slept in a mesquite thicket, shot away all his shells, trying to kill a brush rabbit for his supper—but got the rabbit. It was nearly mid-afternoon now, and there were still about six miles to go; miles that would be double that length, due to the condition of his feet.

But Johnny was used to troubles. He lived with his father, Jim Avery, and his paternal grandfather, Caleb Avery, two hard-bitted rawhiders who had always fought for existence. Jimmy's mother was dead. They had come to Thunder Bird Valley and nested in on land controlled by the Circle C spread, which had ended in a court case, with a decision in their favor. Hank Claybourn had sworn he'd get them off that land, in spite of the law. But they were still there, their brand registered as the AA Connected.

It seemed as though the whole valley was against them, but the two Averys never asked favors. All they wanted was to be left alone to make a living. It wasn't much of a ranch, this AA, and they possessed little livestock.

"Watch the AA, boys," Claybourn had told his men. "Them fellers ain't goin' to eat their own cows. They'll ride with sticky ropes, so watch our calves. And if you get the deadwood on 'em— don't depend on the law."

The Averys heard this. The Circle C owned and controlled most of the valley, so the odds were against the AA. Claybourn was wealthy, while Jim Avery was as poor as the proverbial church mouse. Johnny thought of all this trouble, as he sat there, trying to get the throb out of his feet, before deciding to tackle the last six miles.

The Arizona atmosphere was so clear that he could see the old cliff dweller's homes stretched down the opposite canyon walls, at least two miles away, where the slanting sun etched purple shadows against the rainbow colors of the upper cliffs.

It was all beautiful, but Johnny was not interested in beauty. He was concentrating on his bare feet, which were now very badly swollen.

The wind was blowing across the canyon, as Johnny got up and tested his walking ability, but sat down quickly. On the far side, and around the head of the canyon, a long way off, but plainly visible, were two riders. Johnny could not identify the two riders, but he could certainly identify the two horses, a black-and-white pinto and a coal-black, the two horses that his father and grandfather often rode.

Johnny yelled as loud as he could, but realized that his voice would not carry that far. His gun was empty. Were they hunting for him, he wondered. He waved his hat frantically, but realized they did not see him, as they would have to look almost against the sun.

They traveled in single file along the brushy rim of the canyon, but finally stopped and dismounted. He couldn't see the horses, but he saw the two men against the wall of the canyon, as they climbed down over the broken ledges. Then they disappeared into the broken walls of an old cliff dwelling. It was evident to Johnny that they were not searching for him. But what on earth would they be doing?

It was possibly fifteen minutes later when he saw them again. They came out the same way they had gone in, stopping on a ledge, where they seemed to be looking around. Suddenly one of the men plunged downward, like a man doing a high dive, and a moment later the sound of a shot echoed back against the painted cliffs. Johnny Avery gasped, as his eyes tried to follow the swift plunge of the doomed man.

The other man was scrambling back to the top, and in a few minutes he was riding away, leading the riderless horse, traveling as fast as possible over the broken terrain. Johnny's blood was cold for a moment. He had seen a man murdered in cold blood—and it wasn't nice. He licked his dry lips. Those two men just couldn't be his father and grandfather. Neither of them would shoot the other. At least, Johnny could not conceive such a thing.

Then Johnny forgot his sore feet, and headed for home. It was almost dark when he limped into the old place, coming in from behind the old, tumbledown stable. He stopped short. Something was on the ground near the stable door—a man sprawled in the shadows. Johnny gritted his teeth and walked over there. It was Caleb Avery, his grandfather, and he had been shot to death. The old man clutched a gun in his hand.

Johnny choked and shut his eyes. For moments he was unable to make a move. Then he saw that there was something else up there on the rickety porch of the house. He went up there slowly, fearful, his eyes too misty to see well. He grasped the sagging rail of the porch and looked.

It was his father, flat on his back, arms flung wide. He was dead, too. Johnny knew it. His dad's gun was near him. Johnny picked it up. It hadn't been fired.

There was no way to explain what had happened, but Johnny's one thought was—the Circle C. Hadn't Claybourn sworn he would get rid of them? This was his work.

Johnny went into the house and closed the door. He wanted to think—not look. His whole world was tumbling down, nobody left but him— a kid. He sank down on a bunk and was trying to reason out what to do when he heard horses coming into the yard, voices talking loudly.

But Johnny was range-bred. In spite of the disaster which had come to him, he was still alert to danger. Swiftly he crawled under the bed, his father's gun gripped in his small right hand. Men were on the porch, talking. The door was flung open.

"Why didn't the fools wait for the law to handle it?" a man said. "Takin' the law in their own hands!"

"The boys said they put up a fight, Sheriff," said another man.

"Yeah, I reckon they would—and who wouldn't? The fools—ridin' them two horses to a bank robbery. No brains, Everybody knows them horses. Well, they got Oliver Case—so I reckon it's all right. Saves the expenses of a trial."

* * *

Johnny knew that Oliver Case was the Aztec Wells banker.

"I wonder what became of the kid," said still another voice. "Mebbe they sent him away some'ers, while they pulled the job."

"Smart thing to do, if they did," said another. "The coroner is examinin' the body of the old man, down by the stable, Sheriff."

"All right. We'll load 'em up and get back to town. If the kid shows up, he'll likely come to town."

After a while they went away, and Johnny came out. They hadn't given him much information, but enough to indicate that his father and grandfather had killed the banker and robbed the bank. They had been identified by those two horses—the ones he had seen out at Ghost Canyon—and a posse had shot them down.

But that wasn't true. One of the men who had ridden one of those horses had been murdered at the canyon. It was all very confusing to Johnny, who wasn't old enough to realize that his people had been framed.

It was dark now. He went into the kitchen and found a can of baked beans, but before he could open it he heard more riders. So Johnny went under the bed again.

It wasn't the sheriff this time. Two men came up on the porch, and he heard one of them say:

"The kid ain't here, that's a cinch. If he was, he'd have gone in town with the sheriff."

"Yeah, I reckon yo're right—he ain't come back. But I'd feel a lot safer if he was in the bottom of Ghost Canyon, I'll tell yuh that."

"Along with Nick, eh?"

"Shut up, you fool—and don't name names. We've got to watch out for the kid. Mebbe he was here and saw the shootin'. If he was, mebbe he can prove an alibi for them two dead men. We'll slip back here in the mornin' and have a look. C'mon."

Johnny had heard enough to know that these two men would throw him into Ghost Canyon if they caught him. He found some shells for his gun, after which he ate the beans. Then he pulled a blanket off a bed and made a roll of it, piling in some more canned stuff.

He needed a horse, because his feet were in bad shape. There might be a horse around the place. He went out through the kitchen doorway and there in the moonlight, not twenty feet away, stood that pinto horse, saddled and bridled. The black was not in evidence.

"Paint!" exclaimed the kid huskily. "Paint, you ol' rascal."

The horse came up to him and he picked up the reins. He tied the horse and proceeded to help himself to what he might need. He took his father's gun too; it might come in handy. He wrapped his feet in gunnysack, after putting on a pair of his father's woolen socks, tied his high-heel boots to the saddle horn, and rode away. Johnny Avery didn't know where he was going—but he was heading away from Thunder Bird Valley.

"All a young man needs," his father had often said, "is a good gun on his hip and a good horse between his knees."

Johnny choked as he remembered those words. Jim Avery had been a good father to him—but he was gone now.

"Gotta git m' neck bowed f'r good," whispered the kid. "It's just me and Paint now. So long, Double A. Some day I'll come back here, and when I do I'll betcha the coyotes will have a feed."

Johnny rode only to Ghost Canyon that night. He had a few oats for Paint, a can of beans for himself. He slept on the rim, just above where he had seen those men go down.

Johnny wanted to see what those men had done down there, and why one of them had been murdered.

Next morning at daylight he went down the dangerous trail, where he found the old ruins. The dust was an inch deep on the old floor, and the men's tracks were plain. He found where one of them had been down on his knees, and there, under some broken rocks, he found a canvas sack.

He opened the sack and examined the contents—gold, currency and a little silver. The sack was heavy from the metal. Johnny realized that this was the loot from the Aztec Wells bank. He didn't want any of it.

"It's got blood on it," he whispered. "I've got to hide it."

He made his way along the cliff to another dwelling. Johnny realized that they could trail him in the floor dust, so he didn't go into the dwelling, but worked his way along the upper wall, until he found a crevice big enough to hold the sack. Then he slid a slab of sandstone over the top of it, and went back to his horse.

The sun was just over the horizon as he climbed in his saddle and circled the head of the canyon. He had no destination in mind. He sat in his saddle, his blue eyes thoughtful. Then he spat into the palm of his left hand, struck it sharply with the forefinger of his right hand.

The spittle spurted over his left thumb, and Johnny wiped his palm on his overall-clad knee.

"Straight into the sun," he said aloud. "That's m' orders."

He swung Paint around and headed straight into the sunlight.

CHAPTER 2
Back to Aztec Wells

FIVE HUNDRED MILES FROM AZTEC WELLS, JOHNNY Avery sat on the porch of the Seven K ranch house, facing Bill Keith, the tall, grizzled owner of the spread. Leaning against a post was Tim Boyle, one of Keith's cowpokes. They had been questioning Johnny for quite a while, but the kid wouldn't answer questions.

His horse was not the pinto now, but a gray gelding. Johnny had traded horses twice. Bill Keith studied the red-headed youngster, who was as lean as a greyhound, bleak-eyed.

"Well, yeah—maybe I could use another cowpoke, kid," he said quietly. "But if yuh work for me, you've got to go to school, too. I don't like ignorant cowboys. I'll need yore name to put yuh on the payroll."

Johnny Avery had avoided giving them his name. Now he shut his lips tightly.

"That redhead can pull the blankest face I ever seen, Bill," Tim Boyle said.

Johnny looked up quickly. "You want to know my name?" he asked. "I'm Red Blank."

Bill Keith's eyes twinkled. The kid was quick on the trigger.

"Much obliged, Red," said Bill Keith soberly. "Throw yore bronc in the corral and dump yore bedroll in the bunkhouse—yo're hired."

"Thank yuh kindly," said Red, and headed for the corral.

"I can't figure him, Bill," said Tim, shaking his head. "He can't be more'n twelve years old, but right now he's older'n me and you."

"That's right, Tim," said Bill Keith thoughtfully. "Don't ask him nothin' more. If he wants to tell, he'll tell. Yuh know"—Bill lowered his voice for no reason on earth—"I've allus wanted a kid around the place. Mine died at birth, along with his mother, and I allus wanted one. Maybe this is the answer."

And it was the answer for Johnny Avery, too. He wanted and needed a home, and Bill Keith was like a father to him. His new name was easy to adopt. He forgot that he ever was Johnny Avery. Gradually the hurt of Thunder Bird Valley died away, but Red never told anybody about his past—not even Bill Keith. Red went to the little school until he outgrew the benches.

Bill Keith was a first-class cowman, the fastest man in the country on the draw, and one of the best riders. He taught Red how to make a split-second draw, and to make the first shot count. Red was an apt pupil. He loved bad horses, and in a few years Red Blank's name was synonymous with bronc riding.

Six feet, two inches tall, a hundred and eighty pounds of rawhide muscle, Red Blank feared no man. He was still freckled, but handsome with a flaming mop of red hair and a flashing smile. He was twenty-four now.

His bunkie was "Poison" Oakes, a sharp-faced, skinny-framed cowboy who was always ready for fight or fun. To Poison Oakes, the world was something to laugh at, or with—and how he laughed! Poison was older than Red, and plenty rangewise. He said he had come out of Texas, and fast, but he never explained why.

One day Bill Keith died—broke. Bad investments had swept away his money, and the Seven K spread. Red Blank cried over Bill Keith, the best man he had ever known. Red had saved a little money, and he owned his own horse and riding rig.

The new owners wanted Red and Poison to stay on the Seven K, but they refused. After the funeral the two sat in the bunkhouse, which had been their home for years. "Red, where are we goin'?" Poison said.

"Are you goin' with me?" asked Red.

"Straight into Hades, if you lead the way—and we'll bring out the hot horns of the devil. Whereat have yuh got in mind, Red?"

"Thunder Bird Valley, in Arizona," replied Red quietly.

"Never heard of it," said Poison. "Sounds

kinda good. You got any kinfolks down thataway, Red?"

"Yea-a-ah," breathed Red. "In a graveyard,
Poison."

"Oh! In a graveyard, huh? I see. Well, I'll go
with yuh—but I hope we won't have to visit 'em
permanently."

"It could happen, Poison."

"Uh-huh. Well, you can't figure on livin' always. Let's give her a whirl, Red Feller. How long
since you been there?"

Red was staring at the floor, and it didn't seem
that he heard the question, but finally he said
quietly:

"A million years, Poison, it seems like. But I
reckon it's only about twelve."

"Too long, Red. Pack yore war-sack. It's a
mighty long ride."

And for the first time in his life, Red opened
up and told Poison Oakes what had happened to
him in Thunder Bird Valley. He wanted Poison
to know why he wanted to go back there. The
skinny cowpoke sprawled on his bunk and listened to every word. When the tale was ended,
Poison picked up his war-sack and began shoving
in his belongings.

"Yuh know, Red," he said thoughtfully, "if you
hadn't been so blamed young at that time, I'd say
you'd been a-readin' a book. Before old Tim
Boyle left here he told me how yuh came to the
Seven K. Mebbe yuh didn't read it, feller."

"I couldn't read, Poison."

"I cain't yet—much. Pack yore bag, Red; we're
wastin' time. . . ."

* * *

Alex Trumbull, owner of the Anchor T spread in Thunder Bird Valley, was mad. He also was just a little drunk, too, and not a little dangerous. Alex was the last man to oppose Hank Claybourn's ambition to own or control Thunder Bird Valley, but now, according to Alex, the Circle C had resorted to poisoning his cows.

He had found seven of his cows dead at a waterhole—poisoned. Alex was a pint-sized Scot, about sixty-five years young, shrewd and calculating when sober, but a reckless devil when inebriated. He had fought Claybourn's Circle C for years, refusing to sell out at any price. They said that Alex loved to fight, especially to fight Hank Claybourn.

But "Shorty" Delmar, the grizzled sheriff, was worried. He didn't usually worry about Alex Trumbull, but Shorty had inspected those seven dead cows, listened to assorted opinions from Alex, and then watched Alex drink too much raw whisky. Down in his heart he didn't blame Alex. His herd was far too small to pass over a loss of seven good white-faced cows, and charge it off to experience against the Circle C.

"Lonely" Harte, Shorty's deputy, grinned in anticipation. Shorty didn't like Hank Claybourn.

"Lonely," Shorty said, "you've got to camp on Alex's trail this evenin'."

"Suits me fine," agreed the deputy. "I allus wanted a front seat when Alex turns his hawg-leg on Hank Claybourn—and that danged old *pelicano* acts like he got a itch in his trigger finger."

"Yo're supposed to stop it," said the sheriff severely.

"Yeah, I know, Shorty, but I might be jist a little late. Oh, mebbe a half-a-second too late. How'd that be?"

"Do yore best," replied the sheriff. "Only I hope it don't happen."

"Be just my luck, I reckon."

Lonely leaned against the side of the office doorway and watched two strange cowboys leave their horses at the feed corral. The main street wasn't very wide in Aztec Wells, and the feed corral was almost opposite the sheriff's office.

"Mebbe it's red hair," Lonely said, "but it shore looks like a fire to me."

"What are yuh talkin' about?" queried the sheriff.

"A couple strange cowpokes just left their broncs at the feed corral, and one has the reddest hair I ever seen. He took off his hat and lighted up the street."

Shorty Delmar came over to the doorway and watched Red Blank and Poison Oakes cross the street to the Aztec House.

"Red hair's bad luck," said Shorty. "M' first wife had red hair, and I've hated that color ever since. Can't even wear red drawers."

"Superstition or itch?" asked Lonely.

"It brings back memories. Speakin' of memories, I 'member tellin' yuh to keep track of Alex Trumbull. He's over there in the War Dance Saloon makin' bad medicine for somebody, and he needs watchin', Lonely."

"It's early in the evenin' yet," remarked Lonely.

"Alex ain't brung his tribe up to fightin' stren'th yet, Shorty. Give him time."

"It's yore chore, feller. Try and keep him away from Hank Claybourn and Slim Blake. Hank won't go lookin' for gore, but when Slim hears what Alex's been sayin', he'll boil over."

"Yea-a-ah," sighed Lonely. "Slim's proud of his family tree. If yuh ask me, it's somethin' that his ancestors got hung onto for stealin' cows."

"Yore job is to protect the public, not criticize 'em, Lonely."

"Oh I aim to do that, Shorty. I'll give Alex all the assistance I can, but if two, three men git killed, don't blame me."

"You let Alex do his own shootin', Lonely," said the sheriff severely.

"Oh, shore. Well, I'll start m' vigil. I've done this every time Alex got peevish, and nothin' happened. Tonight won't be no different."

"I hope not," sighed the sheriff, "but I don't feel too happy."

Red Blank and Poison Oakes went to the Aztec House and registered for a room. The old man in charge looked them over curiously, as he fumbled for the dog-eared register. A man came in from the dining room, selected a toothpick from a glassful on the desk, looked at the old man.

"Didja hear about seven of the Anchor T cows bein' poisoned?" he asked.

The hotel man looked up quickly. "No, I didn't, Mike. Is that so?"

"They say it is. The sheriff saw 'em this afternoon. Old Alex is in town, and he swears that

Hank Claybourn will pay him every cent them seven cows was worth, or he'll plumb ruin the census of the Circle C."

"Talk's cheap, Mike."

"Oh, shore. But yuh never can tell. Alex is gettin' organized."

"He mostly allus does, Mike."

The Circle C! The memory of that brand came back sharply to Red. The name of Hank Claybourn, the man who had caused his father and grandfather so much misery. He remembered Hank Claybourn, tall, hard-faced, cold-jawed, riding roughshod over everybody who opposed him. A lot of memories were coming back to Red Blank now.

"Red, I've done asked yuh three times," Poison said. "Do we want a six-bit-a-night room, or a dollar one?"

Red's mind snapped back to realities. "What's the difference?" he asked.

"Two bits," replied the proprietor dryly.

"We'll take the dollar one," said Poison. "I've allus wanted to sleep in a high-class room, one that's been dusted with bug powder."

"Let's go eat first," suggested Red.

"That's right—we're hungry."

"Yore room is Number Seven," said the old man. "Yuh don't need any key—it's open."

They started for the front door, but Red came back to the desk.

"Do yuh know anybody that wants to hire a couple cowpokes?" he asked.

The old man squinted thoughtfully.

"Yuh might ask Slim Blake," he replied.

"Slim's foreman of the Circle C, the one big spread in the valley. They hire quite a few men. Are you two lookin' for work?"

"No," replied Poison quickly, "we ain't."

The hotel-keeper looked curiously at Red.

"Yuh know, there's a difference between a job and work," Poison said.

"Oh, yeah. Well, I don't reckon it'll do yuh any good to see Slim."

They went down to a little restaurant and ate supper. There was some talk in there about Alex Trumbull starting trouble with the Circle C, which made both of them anxious to see something of Alex Trumbull.

"Red, wasn't it this Circle C that made trouble for you?" Poison asked as they left the restaurant.

"From what I can remember, it was, Poison. They tried to run us off, but my dad took it to court and we won. They swore we'd have to get off, and we did—the hard way. The town hasn't changed much. I didn't remember much about it, until I saw it again. It's funny how yuh forget—when yo're a kid. I see faces that I remember, but not the names. That old man was runnin' the hotel, when I was here."

CHAPTER 3
"Fair or Foul?"

THE TWO LEFT THE HOTEL AND WENT OVER TO THE War Dance Saloon.

The War Dance Saloon was a big place, with a lot of gambling layouts. No one paid any attention to Red and Poison when they entered. Alex Trumbull was there at the bar, a skinny little rawhider, bright-eyed as a chicken hawk, but fairly well inebriated. No one was near him.

It was evident that no one wanted to stay too close to old Alex. His remarks about the Circle C outfit were just a bit inflammatory. A cowboy came in and walked casually up to the bar, close to Alex, who paid no attention. The old cattleman was keeping an eye on that big doorway. Suddenly the cowboy reached down, swiftly lifted Alex's six-shooter from his holster and walked quickly away.

For several moments the old man didn't seem to realize what had happened. His skinny right hand swung down to his empty holster, and he whirled, trying to see the man who had taken it. But at that moment "Slim" Blake, foreman of the Circle C, and two of his men came into the saloon, walking directly to the bar. Red Blank recognized Blake, but not the two men with him. Alex Trumbull whirled and faced Blake. It was like a child looking up at a man, but Alex didn't back up. His jaw was set and his eyes blazed.

Big Slim Blake scowled down at the old man, suddenly reached out and grasped him by the neckerchief, twisting it sharply. He threw the old man off balance, then slammed him back against the bar. Old Alex lost his hat, and one of the other men stepped on it.

"Now, you poisonous old pup," snarled Slim Blake, "I'm goin' to make you swallow the words you've been spillin' around town, or I'm goin' to just twist yore dirty old neck right off. Go ahead and talk. Tell 'em you lied, you little skunk!"

"Folks," said Alex painfully. "I said that Slim Blake was a dirty polecat. I'm sorry—and I apologize to the skunk."

"Why, you blasted little, no-good—" began Slim Blake.

"He's pretty small for a man of yore size," said Red Blank, who had moved forward unnoticed by the crowd. "Yo're pretty big to be manhandlin' a little feller—or don't yuh think so? Mebbe that's the size you usually pick out to fight with."

Slim's big fingers loosed Alex, and he turned to stare at Red. Red was a big man, but not as big as Slim, whose hands swung down to his sides as he considered this interruption.

"Just why are you takin' chips in this game, stranger?" asked Slim.

"Oh, just out of curiosity, I reckon," replied Red easily. "I saw how yuh got his gun away, before yuh got brave enough to come in. Yo're a smart man, but you've got an awful mean streak in yuh. And if I'm not color-blind, it's yellow."

"Yellow, eh?" snarled Slim. "Think I am, do yuh? You don't know me."

"My loss, I'm shore," replied Red.

Slim seemed at a loss for just the right words. There was not a sound in the place, as everybody watched. They knew that Slim was a fighter, and they wondered just how good this redhead might be.

"Well?" queried Slim, after a long pause.

"If yo're waitin' for a suggestion," replied Red, "I'd suggest that yuh have the man bring back that gun and give it to the old-timer."

"I'm not askin' you for any advice, my friend, and if you know what is good for you, you'll back up and set down."

Red laughed at him. "Can yuh imagine that?"

Slim's gaze swept up and down the length and breadth of Red Blake. He saw the way Red wore his short holster, and he saw that black-handled Colt, inlaid with a silver wolf's head. Slim Blake's memory flashed back twelve long years. He had seen that gun before. His eyes shifted from that gun to Red's face. Freckles and red hair.

"I hope you'll know me if yuh ever see me again," said Red.

"Lookin' for trouble, eh?" snarled Slim. "Gun trouble?"

"I'd hate to take advantage of yuh thataway," said Red quietly.

"Scared, eh?"

"No, not scared. It's so useless to kill a man you don't even know."

"Turnin' yellow, eh? Don't want trouble? Well, you've gone too far, my red-headed rooster. Shuck that gun, and I'll learn yuh to keep out of my business."

Red swiftly tossed his gun to Poison. Perhaps Slim didn't expect such a ready acceptance to his challenge. He was slow in handing his gun to one of his men, his eyes squinted at Red.

"Do we fight fair—or foul?" Red asked quietly.

"Make it a fair fight," suggested someone. "When a man is down, let him get up."

"If he can," snarled Slim. "All right, Redhead, you wanted it."

They circled away from the bar, and the crowd gave them room. Slim's hands were up in the orthodox fashion, his huge fists clenched, but Red's arms dangled at his sides, his hands unclenched. Red knew the only way for an untrained man to fight was relaxed. Nothing is more tiring than a fighter's stance, especially with clenched fists. For several moments they circled, then Red moved in swiftly, dodging two hard punches, but never trying to land a punch.

Then Slim took the offensive, driving Red back

114

some distance, swinging wildly, but meeting only thin air.

"Stand up and fight like a man!" panted Slim, but Red was playing his own game. He made Slim miss twice more, and he could see Slim's big arms quivering, his mouth open, draining in the smoky air.

Slim missed again and fell into a clinch, both arms around Red, trying to wrestle him down, but Red's right hand was against Slim's throat, and he cut off Slim's wind, forcing Slim to break his hold. And as Slim broke away, he went reeling from a left-handed smash on his right jaw. It was the first blow of the fight that landed, and it did not help Slim in the least.

Slim cursed witheringly and came back at Red, swinging wildly, but the redhead easily avoided punishment and smashed a right fist against Slim's left ear, knocking him against the bar. Slim was hurt, off balance, grabbing wildly with both hands when Red stepped in and drove a smashing right square against Slim's big chin. It was the end of the fight, as far as Slim was concerned. He went to his knees, and then sprawled face-down on the dirty floor.

Red stepped back, and Poison flipped his gun back to him. Red dropped it into his holster, and looked around the room.

"Prettiest punch I ever did see—and plenty hard, too," a man said.

"I'm sorry, gents," said Red quietly. "I don't like to fight. But he kinda had it comin'."

"Where-at is Alex Trumbull?" someone said. "He was here a moment ago."

115

No one seemed to know. The bartender helped one of Slim's men to take him to the back of the room, where they poured water on his head. But Slim recovered quickly. He was still too dazed to know just what had happened, and walked out the back doorway of the saloon alone. He didn't want to talk about it.

The fight was over, and things were getting back to normal when a cowboy staggered into the front of the saloon, minus his hat, and with blood running down his face. Red recognized him as the cowboy who had taken Alex Trumbull's gun. He was dazed and hurt. A man grabbed him.

"Louie, what happened to you?" he exclaimed.

"Trumbull," Louie said shakily. "Dang his hide, he knocked me down with a wagon-spoke and took his gun away from me."

"Where did yuh leave him?" asked Lonely Harte, who had forgotten to follow the old rawhider.

"Leave him?" wailed the suffering cowpoke. "I didn't leave him. He was gone when I got up!"

Shorty Delmar, the sheriff, came striding in. Someone had told him about the fight, and a lot more of them wanted to describe it. Shorty soon had the whole story. Louie Meek was sitting in a chair, nursing his sore head, where Alex Trumbull had hit him.

Shorty sized up Red Blank, who was backed against the bar, one heel hooked over the rail, an amused expression on his face. Beside him stood Poison Oakes, grinning. Shorty grinned, too.

"Anybody know where Alex Trumbull is now?" Shorty asked.

Nobody did. Louie Meek looked up and said:

"Don't worry about him. He's got a wagon-spoke and a gun. He'll get along."

Shorty looked over at Lonely Harte. "Why didn't yuh follow him, like I asked yuh to?" he said.

"With a first-class show goin' on here?" queried Lonely.

"Yeah, I reckon yo're right," sighed the sheriff. "I wish I'd—"

From somewhere came the thudding report of a shot, followed by another. The shots were possibly a second apart.

"Out by the hitchrack!" exclaimed a cowboy. "Anyway, it sounded from that direction."

The crowd moved outside. Several men had come across the street toward the hitchrack. Red and Poison followed the men to the rack, where a man was sprawled in the dirt. Several frightened horses at the rack twisted about, bumping into each other, kicking up clouds of dust.

The sheriff snapped an order for someone to get a doctor.

"Move them broncs away from here!" he ordered.

"Who is it?" asked one of the men anxiously.

"It's Hank Claybourn," replied the sheriff, "and I'm afraid that no doctor on earth can do him any good. Take them horses away—and keep back, until the doctor can look him over. Bring some lanterns, will yuh?"

The crowd moved back, taking away the horses. Hank Claybourn, the biggest cowman in Thunder Bird Valley had been murdered. Red and Poison went back to the saloon. The town was aroused, and there was a search for Alex Trumbull, who was not to be found. His horse was gone.

Investigation showed that Hank Claybourn had been at the Aztec Saloon, playing poker. Someone had told him about the fight at the War Dance Saloon, and one of the boys had told him that Slim Blake had gone home. Claybourn had decided to go home, too, and had been shot at the hitchrack. Louie Meek had been the last one to see Alex Trumbull, and Louie didn't care if he never saw him again.

Red and Poison decided to go back to the hotel, but met Lonely Harte as they crossed the street.

"Boys," the deputy said, "the sheriff asked me to bring yuh down to the office."

"Just what's the idea?" asked Red quickly.

"Oh, it ain't nothin' about that fight," the deputy hastened to assure them. "He was kinda pleased, too."

"All right," said Red, "we'll go down there."

Shorty Delmar was in the office, pulling on a pair of chaps.

"Boys, I don't know either of yore names," he said. "Mine's Delmar—Shorty to you."

"I'm Red Blank." Red smiled. "This is Poison Oakes."

The four men shook hands solemnly.

"I'm glad to meet yuh, Red," Shorty said. "Anybody who can whip Slim Blake is pretty much of a scrapper."

"You didn't ask us down to pin medals, did yuh?" asked Poison.

"No, I didn't, Poison. You boys have heard the talk. It'll spread by mornin'—maybe before—and they'll lynch Alex Trumbull. They've done tried and convicted him. I've got to arrest him and put him in jail, before they get their hands on him. I want to leave Lonely here to throw 'em off the track, and I can't trust anybody around here to go with me. Just hold up yore right hands and take the oath."

"Do yuh mean," asked Poison, "that every time I look in the mirror I'll see a deputy sheriff?"

"Somethin' like that."

"It's goin' to be a dog's life," sighed Poison. "Go ahead."

Shorty forgot the words of the oath, but Red and Poison both said, "We do."

CHAPTER 4
Range Hog's Daughter

Minutes later the sheriff and his new deputies rode quietly out of Aztec Wells, heading for the Anchor T. Shorty Delmar didn't like this job. He had always admired the nerve of Alex Trumbull, and had watched the unequal fight between the Anchor T and the Circle C.

"Of course, you boys don't know anythin' about conditions here," he said. "Alex talked too much, and it looks bad for him, but danged if I can figure that Alex shot Claybourn. Maybe in a fair fight, but not like that."

"Shot twice?" asked Red.

"Uh-huh. Once when he was down. Either shot would have killed him instantly. Whoever shot him shore wanted a complete job."

"Has Claybourn got a family?" asked Red.

"Daughter. Mighty pretty girl, Dale is. Capable, too. Rides like the devil, swears when she gets mad, and breaks the hearts of every cowpoke in the valley. She's twenty, I reckon."

"Interestin'," said Poison. "I've broke a few hearts m'self."

"Candy hearts," added Red soberly. "That's his weakness."

Shorty laughed quietly. "You boys aimin' to stay around here?"

"Just lookin'," replied Red. "The Circle C seems to have all the range tied up, Shorty."

"Yea-a-ah, they have—all except the Anchor T. They say that Claybourn started in here about twenty-five years ago to own the whole valley. Alex had a small spread, which he won't sell. Claybourn started in pickin' up a spread here and there, and about twelve years ago a nester moved in here and filed on the land that the Circle C thought they controlled. It took a court fight to prove he was wrong.

"Well, as they told it to me, this nester and his father stuck up the Aztec bank, killed the banker, and was wiped out by a posse when they was corraled at their ranch house. In some way, Alex Trumbull got this spread. I dunno how, but Claybourn was plenty peeved. There was good water on it. Anyway, Alex rebuilt the ranch house and moved his Anchor T to that spot. Since then, him and the Circle C has been at sword's points. It's been tough goin' for Alex—and it'll be a lot tougher now. Yuh see, he kinda backed them two nesters that was killed, and Claybourn didn't like that either."

"I didn't know that," said Red quietly.

"What did yuh say?" asked the sheriff.

"I mean, I didn't know about the trouble between 'em. I thought maybe it was just some recent trouble."

It was a lame explanation, but the sheriff accepted it.

"Sometimes them old grudges flare up and get awful bad," Poison said.

"This'n did," said Shorty. "Couldn't be worse."

The Anchor T was about an hour's travel from town. Red remembered the old spot among the cottonwoods, but the old house had been torn down and a new one built in its stead.

It required quite a bit of time and knocking on the door to arouse Alex Trumbull. He came with a lamp, his eyes bloodshot, and clad only in his underwear. In his right hand he carried a six-shooter, partly concealed, behind his thigh.

"C'mon in," he said huskily. "I thought it might be some of that blasted Circle C outfit."

He placed the lamp on the table and put his gun aside. Then he got a good look at Red.

"Yo're the feller that knocked Slim loose from the floor, ain't yuh?" he asked huskily. "Much obliged to yuh. Man, you shore impeded him a heap!"

"Yo're welcome," said Red soberly.

Old Alex studied Shorty Delmar for several moments, glanced at an old clock on the wall.

"Well, out with it," he said. "You didn't come visitin'."

"Why did you shoot Hank Claybourn tonight, Alex?" asked Shorty.

The old man stared at the sheriff for a while,

rumpled his hair and both hands, spat dryly and shook his head.

"Mebbe it's just a nightmare," he said. "Say it again, Shorty."

"Somebody shot and killed Hank Claybourn tonight, and they're sayin' you took that gun away from Louie Meek—and shot Hank."

"Sayin' that I . . . Huh! Well, I never done it! I was pretty drunk, but I—" Alex shook his head violently. "Nossir."

"You knocked Louie down and took that gun, didn't yuh, Alex?"

"I shore did, the blasted gun rustler! It was my gun. If it hadn't been for that redhead there, Slim might have hurt me. He was scared to jump me, until his hired help stole m' gun. But I never shot Hank. Not that I wouldn't like to swap lead with him—nossir."

"I'm sorry, Alex," sighed Shorty, "but I've got to put you in the jail until this thing is straightened out. You ain't safe no place else. They're talkin' about a rope and a tree right now."

"They are, huh?" Alex spat and looked around. "Goin' to lynch me for somethin' I ain't done, huh? So yo're arrestin' me for murder."

"I am not," declared Shorty, "I'm puttin' yuh in jail for safe-keepin'. It's my job, and I don't like to do it, Alex, but I'm not goin' to let 'em hurt yuh. You come with me."

"Huh!" Alex snorted. "I can lick that whole gang single-handed."

"Well," said the sheriff soberly, "I'll have to put yuh in jail to save other people's lives then.

Either way, Alex, I've got to put yuh where yuh can't get hurt nor hurt anybody else."

"Well, I'll . . . Huh!" Alex laughed shortly and walked over to his bed, where he picked up his pants. "No use buckin' the law. But"—he stopped and looked at the sheriff—"who's goin' to take care of this here ranch, Shorty? There's chores t' do, cattle to take care of. That is, what's left. If I'm in jail . . . No, I jist can't go to jail, Shorty."

Alex Trumbull tossed his pants on the bed, his mind made up.

"How about me and Poison takin' charge?" asked Red. "We ain't got nothin' else to do, and we don't like to stay in town."

"Huh?" grunted Alex. "You two? I'd like that. I don't know who yuh are, nor where yuh came from, but any man who can whip Slim Blake like you did, I'd shore trust him. Can yuh stay here tonight?"

Red nodded, and Alex put on his pants.

"We'll come in tomorrow and get our war-bags," said Poison.

"I'll leave m' gun with yuh," said Alex. "I won't need it in that jail, and you might need it here."

After they had gone, Red and Poison sat down to consider the situation.

"Well, we shore proceeded to bite off a chunk, Red," Poison said.

"I don't mind it," said Red. "After all, it seems that Alex backed my father and grandfather. I didn't know that. Mebbe I was too young to realize what that must have meant to them. Anyway, it won't hurt us to help him out for a while."

"That's right. And I'll betcha the Circle C will

do a heap of deep thinkin', before they start any trouble with us."

"Things may be different now, since they lost their boss, Poison."

"Let's hope so, Red. I hate trouble. . . ."

After the few simple chores were done around the ranch next morning, Red and Poison went back to Aztec Wells. The town was still excited over the murder of Hank Claybourn. Most of the Circle C outfit were in town. Red met Dale Claybourn on the street with the sheriff, and the sheriff introduced Red.

"This whole thing is mighty sad, Miss Claybourn," said Red. "You have my sympathy."

"Thank you," she said wearily. "You are very kind."

Red thought she was the prettiest girl he had ever seen. Afterwards Shorty said to Red:

"Don't get any ideas, pardner. She's goin' to marry Slim Blake. At least, that's the idea, I've heard."

"Too bad I didn't hit him harder." Red smiled, but added, "Don't get the idea that I'm tryin' to cut him out, Shorty."

"You ain't the marryin' kind, eh, Red?"

"Shucks"—grinned Red—"I can't even take care of myself. I wonder if she knows I had a fight with Slim last night?"

"Yeah, I told her, after you went on."

"I suppose she hates me now."

"Well, I don't know about that, Red. But she smiled for the first time today. Yuh know, her and old Alex have always been friends. It's a fact.

I told her that you and Poison offered to take care of the Anchor T while Alex was in jail. She said, 'Shorty, there are some real folks left in the world after all.'"

"Well, don't she think that Alex killed her father?"

"She didn't say. She only said, 'Shorty, you make Alex as comfortable as possible, because he is a mighty fine old man.'"

"Yuh know," remarked Red, "that girl sounds like she's got a lot of good sense."

"She has," replied Shorty, "and I know she has. I asked her to marry me last year, and she refused."

"She's smarter than I thought," said Red seriously. "But I can't say she's showin' much brains in marryin' Slim Blake."

"That," said Shorty, "shows that yuh can't never tell about a woman. Are yuh comin' up to the inquest, Red?"

"No, I don't think so. Me and Poison will probably go back to the ranch. That jury will hold Alex for the next term of court, and that's all it'll amount to."

"I reckon yo're right, Red. Alex said to tell yuh to look out for Slim Blake. He figures that Slim is a rattler, and won't forget that you humiliated him last night."

Red laughed. "You tell Alex to not worry about Slim Blake. . . ."

Dale Claybourn was weary and heartsick as she sat in the office of David Sanders, attorney-at-law. Sanders had been her father's lawyer for years, and they quarreled like strange dogs. Sanders was about fifty years of age, tall, lean, awkward, proud to have folks say that he looked like pictures of Abraham Lincoln. He leaned over his desk, his eyes closed, hands clasped, as he spoke to Dale.

"The Lord giveth and the Lord taketh away," he said.

"Piety," said Dale quietly, "fits you like overalls on a duck."

"My dear!"

"I've heard things like that all morning. Why do they quote the Scriptures? Dad is gone—maybe to a better place than Thunder Bird Valley. Don't blame it on the Lord."

Sanders shook his head slowly. "You are a queer girl, Dale."

"I try to be honest," she said. "You know, and a lot of other folks know, that my father and I did not get along—not like a father and daughter should. I didn't approve of things he did. I loved him, in spite of it, and—well, he's gone. We might as well be sensible about it."

"Ah, yes—sensible. A great man, Hank Claybourn. Thunder Bird Valley will miss him. Just what did you have in mind, Dale?"

"I want you to defend Alex Trumbull."

"Defend the man who killed your father? Why, Dale, I couldn't do that."

"Did you see him fire the shot?"

"No, I—certainly not! But public opinion—"

"What a lawyer you turned out to be!" said Dale explosively. "What has public opinion to do with it?"

"Well, yes, I—I see what you mean. But as at-

127

torney for the estate, I do not feel . . . Well, you understand, of course."

"Who made you attorney for the estate?" asked Dale.

"Why, I—of course, I have always handled matters for your father, and naturally, I expect to continue."

"That all depends," Dale said quietly. "You have my father's will?"

The lawyer shook his head.

"No, I haven't."

Dale leaned forward quickly. "Where is it?" she asked sharply.

"That is something I do not know, Dale. Less than a year ago he came to this office and asked me to open and read his will, which I did. He said, 'Too long and too hard to understand.' Then he tore it up, saying that he could write a better one. Since that time we have never discussed his will. Whether he ever wrote one, I do not know."

"Suppose there is no will. What happens?"

"You are his sole heir, Dale."

"I see," she said thoughtfully. "I am his sole heir, and still the will you wrote for him was too long and too hard to understand. Why was it so long and so hard to understand, if I was his sole heir?"

"My dear, I am not at liberty to explain the provisions. In fact, I do not remember what they were."

"Lack of memory, eh?"

"Let's not discuss that, Dale. Just be glad if there is no will."

"I think I know what you mean. Will you defend Alex Trumbull?"

"My dear, I am not a criminal lawyer."

"You've done some things that bordered very closely on it."

David Sanders flushed quickly. Long ago he had discovered the futility of crossing swords with this girl.

"We may discuss this later," he said stiffly. "After all, the inquest will decide the necessity of a trial. And why are you concerned over Alex Trumbull? He was your father's enemy."

"My father was *his* enemy, Mr. Sanders. He hated old Alex. Dad has often said that Alex was almost as stubborn as I am. Maybe that is why I like the old man. He fought to save his ranch and for his right to live. I blame Slim Blake as much as Dad. He kept Dad stirred up all the time with tales of what Alex did."

"Your father wanted you to marry Slim Blake, Dale. It was the wish of his life."

"That is too absurd to discuss," said Dale, getting to her feet. "Good day, Mr. Sanders."

"This office is your office, my dear. Come in any time."

"You can have my half for a Christmas present," she said, and closed the door.

CHAPTER 5
A Hard Man's Will

A FEW MOMENTS AFTER DALE CLOSED THE DOOR, SLIM Blake came from the back room of the office, walked over to a window and looked out into the street. Dale was just entering the general store. Slim turned and came back to Sanders. The left side of his face was swollen and discolored.

"Well," said the lawyer dryly, "you wanted to hear what was said, and you heard, Slim."

Slim nodded thoughtfully. "Yeah, I heard," he said. "Did you lie to her about that will?"

"I did not!" replied the lawyer warmly. "Hank Claybourn tore up that will, just as I told her he did."

"And didn't make a new one?"

"How would I know? I didn't make one for him, if that's what you mean. Slim, you may as well forget ever marrying Dale."

130

"That's merely your opinion—and I never did think much of your opinions, Dave. This new deal means that if Hank didn't leave another will I'm sunk, as far as any share of the Circle C is concerned."

"And," added the lawyer rather maliciously, "you are very likely sunk as far as a mere job is concerned. Not such a good outlook, after twenty-five years of work for one spread, Slim."

"You ain't tellin' me anythin' I don't know. . . . Somebody said that them two strange cowpokes are runnin' the Anchor T for Alex."

The lawyer nodded. "The sheriff told me they were. If you want advice on the subject, I'd tell you to let them alone, Slim. Or did you find that out last night?"

Slim laughed shortly. "One swallow don't make a summer," he said. "Mind if I go out the back door? I'd hate to have anybody see me leaving a lawyer's office."

"It might embarrass me, too," said Sanders dryly. "Go ahead, Slim."

Dale went back home that afternoon. She didn't attend the inquest, but she heard that the jury recommended holding Alex Trumbull for trial. The funeral arrangements were all completed, too, and Dale was glad to get away from people and their sympathy, most of which did not ring true.

The Circle C ranch buildings were not exactly pretentious, but the best in the valley. The architecture was a combination of Spanish and cow country, the buildings in good repair, the fences well-kept. Hank Claybourn had a huge steel safe in his room, but Dale did not know the combination nor the contents.

The old Chinese cook, Hop High, had been with the spread ever since Dale was five, had complete charge of the place, and his will was law. He was a little wizened Oriental, sharp of tongue, shrill-voiced, loyal to the core. Hop High came to Dale in the big main room.

"You be boss now," he said.

"I don't know, Hop," she replied. "I went to the lawyer today, but he says Dad tore up his will. Maybe he made a new one, but no one knows where it is."

"Maybeso in safe?" queried Hop.

"Might be." Dale nodded. "But no one has the combination."

"I know how," he said. "Hank show me one time. He say he tlust me."

"You mean you've got the combination, Hop?"

"No sabe what you mean, Missie, but Hop open safe pletty good. I show you."

Dale went with him, and watched the old Chinese twist the dials. It required some time, but finally the big door swung open. It was a very old safe, big enough for a full-time business, but nearly empty now. Dale found a large envelope, sealed, on which was written in her father's hand:

WILL OF HENRY CLAYBOURN

"No open," warned the Chinaman. "Maybeso law not like, Missie."

"Maybe you're right, Hop," she said thoughtfully. "I'll take it to town and have Sanders open and read it."

The Circle C employed ten riders besides Slim Blake, the foreman. They were Louie Meek, Ted Sells, Art Larabee, Tommy Hooker, Bill Morgan, Jim Sharpe, Al Byers, Harry Lane, "Doc" Lee and Jack Peters. Most of them were run-of-the-mill cowpokes.

Doc Lee had been with the Circle C only about six months, and was not the average type of cowboy. Doc was tall, slightly gray, good-looking and seemingly well-educated. He was always polite and courteous, sober, and had never acquired a cowboy dialect.

Doc was an enigma to Dale. He bunked with Slim Blake, and seemed content to draw a cowboy's salary. But the boys said that Doc was fast on the draw, and never seemed to show any emotion.

Dale rode straight back to Aztec Wells and met Shorty Delmar on the street.

"Shorty," Dale said, "I want you to go with me to Sanders' office and listen to the reading of Dad's will. I found it in the safe at home."

"Shore," agreed Shorty. "Glad to do it for yuh, Dale."

They found David Sanders sprawled in his chair, half-asleep, but he awakened quickly. Dale dropped the envelope on the desk.

"I found that in the safe at the ranch, and I brought Shorty to hear it read," Dale explained to the astonished lawyer, who opened it quickly.

He nodded violently as he scanned the page.

"That is your father's writing," he said. "No doubt of that, my dear."

"Nobody has doubted it—yet," she said. "Read it aloud."

Sanders adjusted a pair of reading-glasses, cleared his throat and began. The will read:

> This is my last will and testament. In the event that my daughter, Dale, will marry Slim Blake within thirty days after the reading of this will, she will receive one-half of the Circle C, together with one-half of everything on the Circle C. She shall also receive one-half of all money in my name in any bank.
>
> In the event that she refuses to carry out the above obligation, and does not marry Slim Blake within the specified time, she shall receive five thousand dollars only, and the Circle C, together with everything on the ranch, shall go to Slim Blake. Slim Blake shall also receive all money over the five thousand mentioned above.
>
> Witnessed by R. J. (Doc) Lee
> Signed by
> Henry Claybourn

David Sanders put down the paper and removed his glasses. Dale was staring at the sheet of paper on the desk, her face white.

"Better set down, Dale," Shorty said quietly. "It's kinda hard to take it standin' up."

"I—I can't—" Dale stopped and drew a deep breath. "I can't believe Dad would do that to me," she said huskily. "If I don't marry Slim Blake I lose everything, except a measly five thousand. Sanders, what was in that first will?"

"Substantially the same thing, my dear."

"You mean, I had to marry Slim Blake?"

"I'm afraid you would. Except that the Circle C would be obliged to pay you so much a month for life. Slim could not sell the ranch, and—oh, I don't exactly remember all the provisions. We had quite an argument and I told him he was foolish to not give you everything. After all, he has paid Slim good wages all these years."

"Are yuh shore that's yore father's writin'?" asked Shorty.

"No question about that," said the lawyer, and Dale nodded in agreement.

"I guess that is all," said Dale wearily. "Thank you, Shorty."

They went outside and walked down the street.

"It's too bad Slim didn't go for his gun, when him and Red Blank got into that argument," Shorty said. "It'd saved all trouble over the will."

"Who is this Red Blank, Shorty?" she asked curiously.

"I dunno, Dale. Red just drifted in here. I like him."

"He's fine looking," she admitted, "and he must be all right to take the part of Alex Trumbull, when Slim was going to hurt him. He didn't know Alex."

"Yeah. I think Red is pretty much all right. I think he's from Wyomin'. I was thinkin' today that it's kinda funny we'd turn the Anchor T over to a perfect stranger thataway, but Red's that kind of a stranger. You talk to him for ten minutes, and you feel you've known him a long time."

"Well," sighed Dale, "I must go back home. There are so many things to do, and I don't know just where to start."

"I'm awful sorry about that will," said Shorty. "It wasn't a fair thing to do, Dale, even if it was yore father's work."

"It can't be helped," she said, "but thank you, Shorty."

Shorty and Lonely rode out to the Anchor T that evening, and found Red and Poison finishing their supper. The house was cleaned up, and the mulligan smelled fine. So they sat down and partook of another evening meal, while Shorty told them about the will of Hank Claybourn.

"Hank must have been a real gent," remarked Poison. "Cuttin' out his own flesh and blood to give to a big bully like Slim Blake."

"It shore looks thataway," said the sheriff, helping himself to more stew. "It's shore hard on Dale."

"You've been here a long time, haven't yuh, Shorty?" asked Red.

"About twenty years, Red. I worked several years for the Circle C."

"Did yuh ever know a man whose first name was Nick?"

"Nick? Yeah, I did—Nick Little. He worked for the Circle C about twelve, fourteen years ago."

"What became of him?" asked Red.

"I don't just remember. Probably pulled out. Why do yuh ask?"

"Up in Wyomin' there's a sheepherder whose name is Nick. The boys call him Saint Nick, because of his beard. He don't know what his right name is, except that Nick is part of it. He told me about Thunder Bird Valley, but he's kinda loco on most things. He told me he aimed to come back here some day and shoot the man who killed him."

"Shoot the man who killed him? That's queer, Red."

"It shore is queer. He's always tryin' to remember the man's name."

"The name of some man down here, who killed him?"

"Well, that's what he says, Shorty."

"That's shore funny. He must be crazy. I'll have to tell Slim Blake about that. Him and Nick were bunkies at one time. I can't imagine Nick herdin' sheep."

"Yuh must remember, Shorty—he's dead."

"Oh, yeah, that's right. Poor devil must imagine things. It's a cinch he wasn't killed down here."

"Now ain't that intelligent?" asked Lonely. "How could he have been killed down here that long ago, and be herdin' sheep in Wyomin'?"

"Mebbe," suggested Poison, "it's only his ghost."

"Yuh can't smell ghosts," Red said soberly.

CHAPTER 6
Ghost Story

WHEN THE TWO LAW OFFICERS HAD GONE BACK TO town, Poison asked Red what on earth he had lied to them for.

"You ain't never been in Wyomin', Red."

"It's a good state to lie about," replied Red. "Anyway, Poison, I've got a reason for that lie. There's a few things I never told yuh. For instance, I never told yuh that I saw a man named Nick shot off a ledge on the wall of Ghost Canyon, and that I found a sack of money hidden in an old cliff dweller's home, and hid it in another place. I don't know how much money was in it— but plenty. It was the loot from the Aztec bank, but I was too young to realize it."

"Well, great lovely dove!" snorted Poison. "You've knowed where is a sack of money all these years and didn't go git it, Red? What are we waitin' for?"

Red laughed shortly. "It wasn't my money, Poison—and I don't know just where I hid it. Remember, I was only twelve years old, scared stiff, sick over the whole thing, and it was barely daylight. I've tried to remember what the place looked like, but can't. It was above the wall of an old dwellin', and under a slab of loose rock. Mebbe it's been found long ago, or maybe the rock slid away and the stuff is down among the rocks."

"But didn't yuh come back here to get that money, Red?"

"No, Poison," replied Red quietly. "Like I said before, it wasn't my money. My father and grandfather were killed by a posse of men, who believed they were killers, robbers. Where they were buried, I don't know. I changed my name so that nobody would know who I was. I wasn't ashamed, Poison—I was hurt. And I've always wanted a chance to prove that the posse was wrong—but it's a long time ago and the scent is awful cold."

"Yeah, I can see yore angle, Red. But that sack of money sounds awful good. Nobody would ever be the wiser. It's been forgotten by this time."

"I have a hunch that somebody in this valley remembers it, Poison."

"Mebbe they do, Red. Yuh never forget a sack of money, especially if it ain't where yuh left it."

"One man still remembers it," said Red. "The other was shot off the ledge. I can still see him, spread out like a divin' eagle, divin' for the bottom of the canyon, where he went in among them spearlike treetops. I hope he was dead, before the dive. It must have been awful."

"You still pack yore father's old gun, don'tcha, Red?"

Red nodded slowly. "I've kept it, Poison. It's a good gun, too. It was lyin' beside his right hand, cocked, but not fired. I've never pulled it against a man. Mebbe"—Red smiled whimsically—"I'm keepin' it for the right man."

"I reckon we better go to bed," said Poison. "Next thing I know you'll be tellin' yore right name—and I like the one you've got now."

They buried Hank Claybourn in the little cemetery above Aztec Wells next day. Red and Poison did not attend the ceremony, but went to the cemetery ahead of the others. Red wanted to locate the graves of his father and grandfather, but could not find them. It seemed that all the graves were plainly marked. Nearly everybody in Thunder Bird Valley attended the funeral. Red and Poison sat on a fence and watched the milling throng. Lonely Harte came over and sat with them.

"There isn't an awful lot of graves here," remarked Red.

"This is a awful healthy country." Lonely grinned.

"Is this the only cemetery they've had here, Lonely?"

"This is the only one."

"The Grim Reaper shore ain't had much luck around here," said Poison.

"Yuh know," remarked the deputy, looking at

the distant crowd, "folks are awful hippercrits. There's people over there that hated Hank Claybourn from his belt-buckle both ways—but they've got tears in their eyes. I don't feel thataway about it. If I think a feller is a skunk when he's alive, he still is a skunk when he's dead."

"A funeral sermon even makes a liar out of a preacher," said Red. "He says things that he knows blamed well ain't true. Let's go back ahead of the crowd."

There was a lot of talk in the War Dance Saloon, after the funeral, about Alex Trumbull.

"I believe in an eye for an eye and a tooth for a tooth," one grizzled cowman said.

"Which you're awful shy on," said Lonely Harte.

This brought a laugh, and eased the tension temporarily, but there was talk of not waiting for the law to take its course. Slim Blake stood moodily at the bar, but objected to some of the arguments.

"Let the law handle it," he growled. "After all, you've got to prove a man guilty."

"Don't you believe Alex is guilty?" asked a man.

"I ain't the judge nor jury," replied Slim coldly.

Red and Poison were in there, and Shorty Delmar called to Red.

"Tell 'em what you told me last night about Nick Little, Red."

All eyes turned toward Red, who smiled slowly.

"Well, I dunno much about it, Shorty," he said. "I happened to know an old shepherd up in

Wyomin', who knew his first name was Nick, but he didn't remember his last one. They called him Saint Nick, because of his beard. I got acquainted with the old feller, and he said he remembered somethin' about bein' in Thunder Bird Valley.

"He didn't tell me anythin' about it, 'cause he's kinda loco, and can't remember much, but he said that some day he was comin' back here and kill the man who killed him."

There was not a sound in the room. Men looked at each other curiously. Many of them remembered Nick Little.

"Gosh, that's kinda spooky," a cowboy remarked. "He thought he was dead!"

"Mebbe he is," Red said slowly.

"Dead men don't talk," said another. "How long ago did Nick leave here? He was yore bunkie, wasn't he, Slim?"

Slim Blake nodded, his eyes half-closed in concentration.

"Nick quit and pulled out about twelve years ago," he said slowly. "I never heard a word from him, but Nick didn't have much education, so he never tried to write me a letter. He prob'ly got hurt and imagined all them things."

"Nick must be gettin' pretty old," Lonely Harte said. "He was close to sixty when he left here, and that'd make him seventy, at least."

Red had been watching the faces of the men as he told his lie about Nick Little, trying to detect some sign of consternation, but nothing happened. It was possible that the man who had helped Nick Little rob that bank and kill Oliver Case, the banker, was dead or had left Thunder Bird Valley.

Red and Poison went back to the ranch and cooked their supper.

"You ain't havin' much luck, cowboy," remarked Poison, as they sat down.

"Mebbe Thunder Bird Valley don't believe in ghosts," Red said and smiled.

Poison filled his plate with frijoles, moved the lamp aside and picked up the catsup bottle.

"Yuh know," he said thoughtfully, "the thing to do is to ask old Alex who—"

Crash! The window disintegrated, and from outside came the rattling report of a shot. Poison went backward with his chair. With a sweep of his arm Red flung the lamp off the table, as several more bullets sang a death song through the smashed window. But Red was on the floor, crawling toward the ruined window, gun in hand.

A moment later he heard the drumming of hoofs, as at least two riders raced away.

Red called Poison's name, but there was no answer. It was dark in the room, but Red managed to find another lamp, which he lighted in the main room. He quickly fastened a blanket over the broken window, before turning to the prostrate Poison.

"Blood all over him!" gasped Red. "Poison, speak to me!"

"Have they quit shootin'?" asked Poison.

Red slid back as Poison sat up and mopped at his gore-covered face.

"I—I thought you was dead," faltered Red. "That catsup!"

"Put me between bread and I'd shore make a sandwich," panted Poison. "That whole danged bottle of it hit me in the face. Whooee! Man, that was close! I—I thought I was bleedin' t' death, until some of it ran into my mouth."

Poison managed to wipe most of it off his face, but his shirt was still flecked with red.

"Hungry?" asked Red.

"Not me—not yet. Man, I shore looked death in the face that time! Wasn't there more'n that one shot?"

"Five or six more, I reckon. Well, we'll have to sweep up the glass and mop up the kerosene and catsup."

They cleaned up the place in silence.

"Red, there's somebody around here that don't like me and you," Poison finally said.

"I wouldn't argue against that idea."

"And they'll come back. I wonder who it was."

"I kinda figure," replied Red slowly, "that it's a man who don't believe in ghost stories, Poison. . . ."

Red and Poison went to Aztec Wells next day. Shorty took them in to see Alex Trumbull. The old man was worried, but grateful. Shorty was worried, too. There had been too much talk about the people taking the law in their own hands, and that jail was not built to stand a siege.

Red told them about the attack at the ranch. Shorty was amazed that anybody should attack them. No reason for it.

"It's that blasted Circle C, I tell yuh!" Alex said.

144

"They're killers. They've tried everything for years to get me off that place. If—well, if anything happens to me, I'll betcha the Circle C will get it."

"Why would the Circle C try to kill Red and Poison?"

Red told Alex to not worry about the ranch. Back in the office Red and Shorty talked things over. Red mentioned the will of Hank Claybourn.

"Yuh know, I don't believe Slim knows about that will," Shorty said. "I told you and Poison, but outside of that I believe that Dale, Sanders and me are the only ones who know what was in it. Dale was shore honest. She took it to the lawyer to have it opened. If it'd been me, I'd have read it and burned the blamed thing."

"It would have saved the ranch for her, if she had," said Red. "I wonder if she kept the will."

"No, I think the lawyer has it, Red. He put it in his safe, before me and Dale went out. She wouldn't want it, that's a cinch."

"In the lawyer's safe, eh?" mused Red. "Yuh know, I've seen that slab-sided Sanders, and I wouldn't trust him as far as I could drop-kick a range bull."

"I reckon he's honest enough," said Shorty, "but he always has been a pretty good friend to Slim Blake."

"That sinks him for the last time," declared Red. "See yuh later."

CHAPTER 7
Disappointed Lynchers

DALE CLAYBOURN HAD NOT TALKED WITH SLIM BLAKE about the will. In fact, she wasn't interested in even discussing things with him. The provisions of the will had been a great shock to her, and she did not want to talk about it. Just why on earth her father would do such a thing was beyond her, although she realized that Slim had dominated him in many things.

She was upstairs in her room, late that evening, when she heard a door close quietly downstairs. Hop High never came into the main room after supper, unless sent for. The sound made Dale curious. She went quietly to the top of the stairs, from where she could see her father's room. The door was partly open, and there was a faint illumination.

Softly she went down the padded stairway and

toward the rear of the room, which was in darkness, except for that faint glow. Someone else came into the room, and Dale crouched quickly in against one end of the huge fireplace, as this newcomer came silently. His bulk shut off the glow.

"Hold like you are, Doc!" Dale heard him say.

It was Slim Blake's voice, talking to Doc Lee.

"Put down that gun, Slim," Lee said quietly.

"That's yore idea. I expected this, Doc. When you argued that you wanted a better deal, I kept an eye on yuh. So you were goin' to get that will and hold it over me, eh? I'm not crazy. All right, open the safe—and I'll take charge of it. Go ahead and open it."

There was silence for several moments, and then Slim said:

"Where is it? Gone, eh? Doc, you dirty coyote, you! Go on—talk."

"Don't be a fool, Slim," said Doc Lee. "If it wasn't here, and I knew it, why would I be openin' the safe? Use your brains, Slim. And as far as gettin' a new deal—you better do it. No, I'm not afraid of yore gun."

"But where's the will? Dale didn't know the combination. One of us had to take that will out of that safe, and I didn't do it."

Dale forgot the extreme danger she was in, walked over and shoved the door wide. Both men whirled at the sound, and Slim's gun covered her. It was an embarrassing situation.

"So you two are making deals on my father's will?" Dale said. "Fine. Now, just for your own information, I did open that safe, took out the will and turned it over to Mr. Sanders."

Doc Lee got slowly to his feet. Dale was mad, but foolish.

"I'm going to have both of you arrested for attempted burglary," she declared. "And then you might tell us a few things about that will, and why you both wanted a deal of some kind."

"You're an awful little fool," snarled Slim. "Why didn't yuh keep yore nose out of this?"

"Don't you point that gun at me," said Dale angrily.

"Doc," Slim said, "you take yore gun and keep her here, until I get back."

"Where are you goin'?" asked Doc Lee.

"I've got to see a lawyer about a paper."

"Do I get my right cut, Slim?"

"Yuh do, if things break right. Watch her."

"Do you think you can get away with high-handed things like this?" asked Dale furiously. "The law will have something to say!"

"The law won't be consulted, sister," said Doc Lee. "Sit down and stay down."

Slim went swiftly down to the stable, saddled his horse and headed for Aztec Wells.

"Yuh might as well relax, sister," Doc Lee said to Dale. "We'll be here quite a while."

"I don't understand what this is all about," she said.

"You'll know the answer later—and you won't like it, miss. Young ladies are to be seen and not heard. . . ."

* * *

Things were not exactly normal in Aztec Wells. Red and Poison had surveyed the place that evening and decided that something was going on. Men talked in small groups, being careful to speak quietly and to cease all conversation upon the approach of anyone.

Red and Poison did not go to supper until about ten o'clock. They had not seen Shorty Delmar or Lonely Harte for several hours, but while they were eating Lonely came into the little restaurant. He was not hungry, but he was apprehensive. Lowering his voice he asked if they had seen Shorty. They had not.

"I'm a-gettin' jumpy," declared Lonely. "Too much private conversation. I'm like a scared pup—I can't make the hair on m' neck stay down."

"Why don'tcha get a neck-shave?" asked Poison.

"That might help. I've got to go back to the jail. If yuh see the sheriff, tell him to come down there right away."

They promised to do that. After their meal they walked back to the front of the hotel, where they sat down. Several men sauntered past them casually, but Red realized that they were being looked over.

It was about ten o'clock when Slim Blake rode slowly into town and tied his horse at the War Dance hitchrack. But instead of going to the hotel, he went straight to the office of David Sanders.

The office was dark, and no one answered his knock on the door. He tried the door and found

149

it unlocked. He went in, closed the door and lighted a match. What he saw caused him quickly to light the lamp on Sanders' desk. David Sanders was lying on the floor, close to his half-opened safe, tied hand and foot, and gagged with a dirty towel.

Slim quickly tore away the gag and took off the ropes. Sanders was unhurt, but boiling over. As soon as he was able to talk, he told Slim that a masked man had stuck him up as he had come from his stable, forced him to unlock his safe, and then tied him up.

Slim squatted on his heels and listened to Sanders' story. The floor in front of the safe was littered with papers.

"What'd he want out of yore safe?" asked Slim anxiously.

"I don't know," whined the lawyer. "I'll have to check all my papers, before I can tell."

"All right," said Slim coldly. "Did you have Hank Claybourn's will?"

"Yes, I did. Wait! It should be easy to find out if it's here."

But the will was not there. Sanders leaned back against the safe door and looked blankly at Slim, who licked his lips and stared at Sanders.

"All I've got to say is this," Slim said. "You get it back."

"But I don't know who got it, Slim."

"I want it back," said Slim coldly.

"Maybe—Doc?"

"Doc didn't get it. Tonight I caught him tryin' to find it in Hanks' old safe. I want it back, Dave—and blasted soon, too."

Slim went outside and closed the door. As he started for the War Dance Saloon, a man stepped out of the shadows.

"Slim," he said, "we're glad yuh came in. In about fifteen minutes we're goin' to save some money for the county."

"Yuh mean yo're going to—tonight?"

"That's right. We've blocked off both roads into town. We'll circle around the livery stable and meet the boys out there."

"Where's Shorty Delmar? He'll put up a fight."

"He's tied up in the feed stable. We've had him all evenin'."

"Good. I feel like havin' some fun. Let's go."

Red and Poison still sat in front of the hotel. They saw Slim and this other man pass the lights of the War Dance Saloon, and disappear in the darkness.

"There's trouble ahead," Red said, "and it's comin' awful fast. Poison, mebbe me and you better hightail it around to the jail and help Lonely, unless he's smart enough to get under cover."

Poison turned his head and saw Lonely in the hotel doorway. The deputy recognized them and came out.

"Lonely," Red said, "don't yuh realize that they're framin' to smash yore jail and lynch that helpless old man?"

"Yeah, I figured that out early this afternoon, Red."

"And you've left him to their tender mercy?" asked Poison. "They'll hang him higher'n a kite."

"If they can catch him," amended Lonely, sitting down.

"What do yuh mean?" asked Red quickly.

"Nothin' much—except that I turned him loose an hour ago. He's got his own gun and my horse, and he shore knows the country."

"Lovely dove!" snorted Poison. "Lonely, that's illegal!"

"So's lynchin'," replied Lonely dryly. "They'll prob'ly arrest me for doin' it, but I don't care. I couldn't stop 'em, so I fooled 'em."

"I think I'd like to shake hands with yuh, Lonely," said Red.

"Much obliged. Let's take a seat at the show and see what happens."

They followed Lonely around the hotel and he led them to an old board fence, about a hundred feet from the jail. There was no moon, but the starlight was bright. Two men came in from behind a building and walked close to the jail, circling it completely. Then came a compact body of men, carrying a plank.

There was no conversation, until one man gave the order. A moment later the front door crashed open.

"We'll have to git that door fixed tomorrow," Lonely said.

They were in there a short time, and all came out. One of the men cursed Lonely Harte, but the others were silent, as they made their way back to the street.

Red, Poison and Lonely went back to the front of the hotel. The War Dance Saloon was full of men, drinking at the bar. It was about fifte minutes before Shorty Delmar came up the street.

Shorty was mad, humiliated and curious. Two masked men had let him loose, but didn't tell him what happened. He had gone to the jail and found the front door smashed, but all cells locked.

"What happened, Lonely?" he asked huskily. "Did they—get him?"

"Not unless he went awful slow," replied Lonely.

Shorty gave his deputy a sharp look.

"What do yuh mean?"

"I mean I turned him loose, Shorty, and gave him a gun and a horse."

"You—well, I'll be danged! You turned . . . I'm glad, Lonely, glad to have a deputy with that much sense."

"It wasn't brains—it was laziness, Shorty. It's a heap easier to turn a man loose than it is to fight twenty men at once."

"We'll both probably lose our jobs, Lonely."

A man came across the street to the hotel. It was David Sanders.

"Sheriff," he said, "I've been looking for you. A masked man held me up at my office, made me open the safe, and then tied me up. He gagged me, too. It was awful! He threw all the papers out of my safe."

"Did yuh get a good description of him?" asked Shorty.

"He was masked, I tell you!"

"What color mask?" asked Lonely, but the lawyer ignored him.

"What did he take from yore safe, Dave?" asked Shorty.

"The will of Hank Claybourn."

"The will of . . . Well, what good would that do anybody?"

"It isn't filed, and there is no copy."

"That's awful careless of you, David," Lonely said chidingly.

"Well, great Scott!" snorted Shorty. "What'll happen next?"

"I hear Alex Trumbull broke jail tonight," said Sanders.

"He did not!" snapped Lonely. "I turned him loose."

"I—I was supposed to defend him," faltered the lawyer.

"You?" gasped Lonely. "Why, you can't even defend yourself, Dave."

"I believe you are right. Good evening."

David Sanders turned around and hurried back across the street.

"He gave yuh good evenin', Shorty," reminded Lonely.

"Yeah, he's generous. Lonely, you say yuh gave Alex a gun?"

"It was my own gun, Shorty. I gave him my gray horse, too. I can't find use for more'n one horse and one gun."

"You'll prob'ly need more than one, when the citizens of this here fair valley find out you turned a murderer loose and gave him a gun."

"And a horse, too," added Lonely. "And don't forget that a lot of the good citizens was hangin' onto that plank, which ruined the front door of the jail. I could have been a hero, I reckon. I could have barred the door, stood inside and defied 'em. Mebbe I could have killed fifteen, twenty of 'em, before I died. Mebbe they'd have put up a monument to me on the main street, but I'd a heap rather be forkin' a horse, hightailin' it out of the country, and be knowed for a coward and a bad officer, than to . . . I wonder if the dead can look back and see the monuments folks put up in their honor?"

"No," said Red with great finality. "A good and wise Providence prevents them from further embarrassment."

"Uh-huh. Well, Shorty, if yuh don't mind, I'll ride out and stay all night with Red and Poison. Aztec Wells ain't healthy for me tonight."

"I'll go along," said Shorty. "There's nothin' more in the jail we can lose."

CHAPTER 8
Thumb Print Clue

ON THEIR WAY OUT TO THE ANCHOR T, RED ASKED Shorty if he had any idea who the men were who held him captive in the stable.

"Yeah, I knew some of 'em," replied Shorty. "Good citizens, too. At least, they're suspected of bein' good citizens."

"Was Slim Blake one of 'em, Shorty?"

"I didn't see him, Red, but I heard a man whisper that Slim was with 'em."

They soon discovered that Alex Trumbull had been at the ranch. A scribbled note propped against a lamp said:

TOOK BLANKETS, GRUB AND A RIFLE. —ALEX.

"I'm shore glad the old man stocked up," said Lonely.

"Yeah"—Shorty nodded, "and I'm not wastin' my time tryin' to find him either. They can fire me off the job, if they want to. Yuh know, it's awful funny about somebody robbin' Sanders of that will."

"Yeah, it is," agreed Red thoughtfully. "I wonder why it was done. That will wouldn't be any good to anybody, except Dale and Slim."

"Mebbe somebody wants to make Slim pay through the nose," suggested Lonely. "Without that will, Slim's stuck."

"Suits me," said Shorty. "He wasn't entitled to the Circle C, anyway."

Red and Poison had covered all the windows with blankets, fearing a return of the men who had almost killed them through the kitchen window. Nothing happened that night.

Next morning Shorty and Lonely went back to town to face what music might be played. Red and Poison saddled their horses and rode out toward Ghost Canyon. Red had never been out there since leaving Thunder Bird Valley, and he wondered if he could remember places and things.

They rode the north rim, and Red thought he had found the place where he had been sitting on a rock, nursing his sore feet, when he had seen a man murdered across on the other rim. They left their horses and walked to the rim, where they sat down, while Red studied the old cliff dwellings, and tried to remember exactly where the tragedy had occurred.

Suddenly Poison pointed across the canyon.

"There's a man over there, Red! See him? Climbin' down over a ledge. Over there, to the right of the first cave."

Red saw him, working his way down the side of the cliff. As well as Red could remember, it was the same ledge from which another man had plunged to his death. This man had reached the ledge and was standing up straight.

"He's got somethin' in his arms, Red," Poison said. "There it goes!"

The man had tossed something off the ledge, which fell swiftly into the depths of the canyon. What it was, they could not see, but it flashed red in the sunlight, which slanted down the side of the cliffs.

"Looked like it might be a red shirt, with a rock tied to it," Poison said quietly.

"Red shirt, with a rock tied to it? By golly, it did, at that! But why on earth—"

Red stared into the canyon, a scowl on his face. Suddenly he laughed, and slapped Poison on the back.

"What's eatin' you?" asked Poison quickly.

"The ghost of Nick Little!" exclaimed Red. "That story I told of the shepherd in Wyomin', Poison. That red shirt is a marker. If the bones of Nick Little ain't down there—and he threw a marker. If he can find that red shirt, he'll be awful close to where he threw Nick Little, or where Nick fell off the ledge, after this man shot him."

"Lovely dove!" gasped Poison. "I'll betcha that's it!"

"But where's the man?" asked Red.

In their excitement they had lost track of him. They sat there quietly for possibly fifteen minutes, but there was no sign of the man over there, so they decided that he had climbed back to the rim. Poison wanted to go into the canyon and see if they couldn't run into the man.

"And run slap into hot lead, eh?" said Red. "That hombre prob'ly knows the canyon, and we don't. Anyway, we've got him worried."

"Do yuh reckon there'd be anythin' left of Nick Little, after all these years, Red?"

"Could be. That's pretty deep for buzzards, and this country is awful dry. I hope the man comes back and tells me I'm a liar."

They went back to the ranch, but decided to go on to Aztec Wells. Red was curious to find out what the reaction over the escape of Alex Trumbull might be.

They found David Sanders, the lawyer, in the sheriff's office, talking with the sheriff and Lonely. Sanders had been out to the Circle C to talk with Dale, but she was not at the ranch. Hop High was excited. Dale hadn't slept in her room, and the old Chinese was worried.

Pinned on her pillow they had found a note, which Sanders had just given to the sheriff. It read:

HAVE GONE AWAY FOR A WEEK OR TWO. DON'T LOOK FOR ME. —DALE.

The sheriff handed it to Red, who looked it over carefully. It was written in pencil on a piece of pink-tinted paper.

"Who took the paper off the pillow, Sanders?" Red asked.

"Why, I did. I don't see what that matters."

"Hop High didn't touch it, did he?"

"No, he didn't, but I don't see what you're getting at."

"Let me look at yore thumb, Sanders—the left one."

Somewhat mystified, the lawyer exhibited his thumb. In fact, Red took a look at both thumbs. Then he examined Shorty Delmar's thumb.

"If yo're making a collection, here's mine," Lonely said.

"You didn't handle that note, did yuh, Lonely?" asked Red.

Lonely shook his head. Red smiled as he laid the note on the desktop and pointed to a decided smudge on the paper, made by a rather big and evidently quite soiled thumb.

"That wasn't made by a woman," he said quietly.

"I never noticed that before," said Sanders. "Why, it is all clean, except for that."

"It's because the man held the note in his left hand when he pinned it to the pillow, and his thumb was dirty."

"But I'd swear it is Dale's writing," said the lawyer.

"Well, what does it mean?" asked the sheriff. "If Dale didn't write it, what's happened, Red?"

"That is something to be found out, Shorty."

"But it is Dale's handwriting," insisted Sanders.

"Mebbe she went away with a man," suggested Lonely.

"And gave him the note to pin on the piller," added Poison.

"Dale wouldn't go away with any man," said the sheriff.

"Not voluntarily," amended Red.

"You mean she was forced to go with him?" asked Sanders.

"What do *you* think?" asked Red pointedly.

"I have no theory. I took the note at its face value."

The lawyer went away. Shorty Delmar sank down in his office chair and wearily rolled a cigarette.

"The commissioners came to visit us this mornin'," Lonely said.

"And," added Shorty, "we've got to have old Alex back under lock and key within twenty-four hours, or resign."

"That'd be quite a chore," remarked Poison.

"And they didn't give me no credit for blockin' a lychin'," said Lonely. "If I hadn't turned him loose, he'd be dead now, but they don't seem to care about that."

"I'm not interested in Alex," said Shorty, "and I'm not anxious about this job—but I'd sure like to know what happened to Dale."

The note was still on Shorty's desk. Red picked it up and read it again. It seemed genuine enough, and the paper was pink-tinted, such as a woman might use for short correspondence.

"Yuh don't see much paper like that," remarked Poison.

"That's an idea," said Red. "C'mon, Shorty."

The elderly postmaster examined the paper carefully.

"It's kinda funny," he said. "I had a little box of that color paper and it disappeared. I know blamed well I never sold it."

"Didn't Dale Claybourn buy it?" asked Red.

"No, she didn't. She always bought the blue kind. I missed that box of pink paper last week."

Red and Shorty went back to the office. Shorty was more worried than ever now.

"Somebody stole that paper, Shorty," Red said, "and they forged that note. They forged . . . Wait a minute! By golly!"

"What's eatin' yuh, Red?"

"An idea. I can't tell yuh what it is, but it's an idea. C'mon."

They went over to David Sanders' office. Sanders was at his desk, and he eyed them narrowly.

"You told us that a masked man tied you up and robbed your safe last night, Sanders, and that he took the will of Hank Claybourn," Red said.

"That's right," said the lawyer, tight-lipped.

"Who turned yuh loose, Sanders?"

"Why, Slim Blake. I thought I told you that."

"Why did Slim Blake come to your office?"

"I—why he didn't say. I suppose he was upset and forgot to say."

"What *did* he say?"

"Wait a minute," said Sanders testily. "What right have you to ask me questions? After all, these things are none of your business."

"They're mine," said the sheriff, "and Red's askin' for me."

Sanders glared at Shorty, but replied evenly:

"I don't remember what he said. I was too upset to pay attention."

"As a matter of fact," said Red, "that will was forged."

"Forged?" Sanders forced a laugh. "Well, maybe it was, but who can prove it?"

"It don't have to be proved—it's gone. That note signed by Dale's name was forged. Somebody stole that writin' paper from the post office, Sanders. Whoever forged that will, forged that note from Dale."

"You've found out that much, Blank—why don't you find Dale? You can't prove the note is forgery, except through her. And you can't prove the will is a forgery, because Hank Claybourn is dead. Yours is only a tempest of theory. I hope you are right. If it is a forgery, it is a clever forgery—and who in Thunder Bird Valley has talent in that direction? Not Slim Blake. He can hardly sign his own name."

"Mebbe I'm wrong," sighed Red, "but I don't believe I am."

"I'd like to know this," said the sheriff. "Somebody stole that will from yore safe, Dave. Outside of Dale and Slim Blake, who would steal it? It's a cinch Dale didn't steal it, and Slim wouldn't have any cause to steal it. This deal don't make sense."

"It does not," replied the lawyer firmly, "and I'd like to get my hands on the man who forced me to open my safe."

"What would you do to him?" asked the sheriff curiously.

"I—I don't know—exactly,' admitted the lawyer. "It was just an idea."

"I hope you do," Red grinned. "I'd like to see what happens."

As Red and the sheriff crossed the street from Sanders' office nine riders came into town. With the exception of Slim Blake and Doc Lee, it was the whole crew of the Circle C. They tied up at the War Dance Saloon, and Louie Meek came across the street and joined them.

"Startin' on a roundup, Louie?" asked the sheriff.

Louie Meek laughed shortly and shook his head.

"Slim Blake fired the whole gang," he said. "All that's left out there is Slim, Doc and Hop High."

"What happened?" asked the sheriff.

"Well"—Louis took off his hat and mopped his forehead—"it all started over an argument. We didn't like the deal Dale was gettin'. Yuh know she pulled out, didn't yuh? Well, we had an argument at breakfast. Slim got kinda runty and said he owned the Circle C, and as far as Dale was concerned, she could go to the devil. Bill Morgan told Slim what he thought of him, and it almost caused shootin'. We all backed Bill's play, and Slim fired every blasted one of us."

"How come that Doc Lee and Hop High didn't get fired?"

"Well, Lee didn't mix into the scrap, and Hop High got himself a cleaver."

"Where do yuh reckon Dale went, Louie?"

"We thought mebbe she stayed here in town, Shorty."

"I don't believe she did. Is Slim at the ranch now?"

"He was there when we left, Shorty."

Louie went into the general store.

"Red, I believe I'll go out to the Circle C and have a little talk with Slim Blake," Shorty said.

"I believe I'll go with yuh," said Red, and grinned. "Poison can stay with Lonely, in case any criminals want to give themselves up."

CHAPTER 9
Cliff Dwellers

SANDERS, THE LAWYER, WAS COMING FROM THE POST office when the sheriff called to him. Sanders didn't seem too happy.

"Dave," said the sheriff, "Slim Blake fired nine of his cowpokes this morning."

"Indeed!" grunted the lawyer. "Fired nine of them, eh?"

"What I want to know is this," said the sheriff. "Has Slim Blake got the right to do a thing like that?"

Sanders shook his head slowly. "Ownership of the Circle C has not been determined, Sheriff. That will has not been filed. In fact, as far as the law is concerned, there is no will. In my opinion, Slim Blake has no right to be operating the Circle C. Under present conditions, the law would

165

only consider Dale Claybourn as being in charge."

"Much obliged, Sanders."

The two men had no plans as they rode out to the Circle C. Slim was there, sitting on the board porch of the ranch house, and he looked narrowly at the two men as they dismounted. Slim had no love for either of them, especially for Red Blank.

"Ridin' or goin' someplace?" asked Slim, trying to be cordial.

"Stoppin' here, Slim," replied the sheriff. "I talked with the boys in town, and they said you fired all of 'em."

"That's right," replied Slim grimly.

"Actin' a little sudden, wasn't yuh?"

"Oh, I dunno, Shorty."

Shorty Delmar leaned against the porch railing, his eyes thoughtful.

"Yuh see, Slim," he said, "you've been takin' a lot for granted. After all, you don't own the Circle C. There's no will, nothin' to show that you own it, and the law considers Dale the owner."

"Oh, is that so?" sneered Slim. "You know well enough there was a will."

"Was and is are two different words, Slim. The law only considers what it sees, not what it hears about."

"Yea-a-ah?" Slim shifted his eyes to Red. "What's yore put-in on this deal, Red?" he asked.

"Oh"—Red smiled—"I just came along to tell yuh that we're askin' the boys to all come back on the job, and havin' the law appoint a man to run the Circle C until Dale Claybourn comes back to run it herself."

"Oh, yuh did, did yuh? Well, ain't that nice! And what'll I be doin'?"

"Lookin' for another job, I reckon."

Slim Blake was mad, but apprehensive. He realized that it could be done.

"I suppose Sanders told yuh that, the dirty pup," he said.

Red slid under the rail and came up almost behind Slim, who shifted quickly.

"Set still, Slim!" Red said. "We ain't goin' to hurt you, if you do what I tell yuh to do."

"What's that?" growled Slim.

"Call over to the bunkhouse and tell yore watchdog to lay down that Winchester and come out here. We don't like to get plugged in the back. Yeah, I saw him. Start callin'."

The door of the bunkhouse was slowly closing, but opened when Slim called:

"Doc! It's all right!"

Shorty Delmar drew a deep breath, his eyes narrowed.

"What was you expectin', Slim?" he said.

"Yuh never can tell."

"All right, Slim," said Shorty. "We're goin' back to town and get an order from the court to take over the Circle C. When you find that will and get possession through law, we'll move out and let you in. Until that time, Dale Claybourn owns this place—and the law protects it. Yuh understand what I mean, Slim?"

What Slim replied was strong, but he was powerless to do anything about it. He looked at those two men and realized that any false move on his

167

part would start trouble—and Slim Blake didn't want any trouble with the law.

"We're sendin' the boys back," said Shorty, "and they might not be in good humor. In fact, if I was you, I'd be awful scarce."

"Some day, Shorty, you'll be sorry for this," gritted Slim.

"Oh, I've got a lot of things to be sorry about, Slim. But I'll take 'em as they come. *Adios*."

As they rode back to Aztec Wells, Shorty said:

"Red, I didn't see that reptile down there in the bunkhouse with a Winchester."

"Neither did I," said Red, "but I thought I'd play safe."

Red and Poison slept in the hayloft that night. Next morning Red left Poison at the ranch, and rode to Ghost Canyon alone. He wanted to try and remember where he had hidden that loot from the Aztec Bank. He tied his horse on the rim and sat down, trying to remember just where he had gone that morning over twelve years ago.

There was the ledge down a ways, where a man had been thrown into the canyon, and where another man yesterday had flung some red-looking object. He climbed down there and made his way into the first of the old cliff dwellings. They were pretty much all alike, mostly roofless, with broken walls, the old floors deep in dust and rubble.

Red remembered the tracks in the dust, which led him to the money cache, but more of the walls had collapsed, it seemed. He leaned on a shelf of the broken masonry and tried to remember just where he had gone after he had found the money.

"Don't move," a voice snapped suddenly, "or I'll blast yuh!"

Red flinched, but did not turn, and his hands slowly lifted. Something struck him on the head, and he went to his knees, dazed, half-knocked out, powerless to help himself for the moment. He tried to draw his arms away, but they were forced behind him, and roped quickly. Then a man twisted Red around, and he blinked up at a masked figure, standing over him with a gun.

Red's head was fairly splitting, and the sunlight in his eyes was painful. The man laughed harshly.

"Stuck yore nose right into it, eh, Redhead?" he said.

He had Red's old gun, looking at it curiously.

"Silver wolf head, eh? Well, yore fangs are drawed, my friend."

He helped Red to his feet, but Red was a little unsteady.

"What's the idea?" asked Red painfully.

"You'll find that all out in a short time. Head straight out that broken place over there, and don't do any foolin', because it's a thousand feet into that canyon—and I don't want to lose yuh—yet."

He herded Red out onto a narrow shelf where broken ledges led downward toward another old dwelling, which seemed to be suspended over the canyon, with little visible means of support."

"Lean in against the wall," warned the man, "and watch were yuh put yore feet."

Red obeyed as well as possible, but his head ached badly, and he was unable to balance himself, with his arms tied behind him. They came in under an overhang of rock, where the shelf ended. A huge old manzanita grew out of a crevice at the end of the ledge. Straight below, and about thirty feet down, was another ledge, which led to the broken entrance of the old dwelling.

From under the manzanita the man drew a big coil of half-inch hard-twist rope, which he proceeded to knot under Red's shoulders. Then he took a dally around the butt of the big manzanita.

"All set, Red," he said sharply. "Set down and slide over the edge. I'm lowering yuh to that ledge down there. You'll either do as I tell yuh, or I'll bang yuh on the head again. Either way, yo're goin' down. And when yuh get down there, don't get any ideas, feller. That's the end of the trail—and this is the only way out."

Red slid down, twisting with the rope, as the man lowered him to the ledge. Then the man flung out a rope ladder, and came down quickly. He untied Red, helped him to his feet and drove him through the entrance to the dwelling. Dale Claybourn was there, propped against the rubble, tied hand and foot, but seemingly uninjured.

The masked man shoved Red down near her, and quickly tied his feet. Breathing a sigh of relief he went back to the entrance and stared off across the canyon.

"Howdy, Ma'am," said Red. "Are yuh all right?"

"I think so," replied Dale quietly. "You are Red Blank?"

"Yes'm. Nice weather we're havin'."

The masked man turned and looked at them closely, but said nothing. Then he went back on the ledge and disappeared.

"They haven't hurt yuh, have they, miss?"

Dale shook her head.

"No, I haven't been hurt—and my name is Dale."

"I'm Red." He grinned. "Might as well admit it, since I lost my hat."

"Does anyone know where I am?" she asked.

"Not a soul. I mean, nobody except them that brought yuh here, and they don't rate a soul, anyway. You left a note, pinned on yore bed at home, sayin' you'd be away for a couple of weeks."

Dale's tired eyes opened wide. "I never left any note, Red!"

"Somebody did, and Sanders swears it's yore writin'."

"It wasn't. I never wrote any note."

"Why on earth did they bring you here, Dale?"

"Slim Blake swears that I have that will. He says that either Dave Sanders gave it to me, or I hired somebody to steal it from Sanders' safe. He says he is going to make me tell him where it is."

"Slim Blake is a right sweet character," said Red soberly. "Yesterday he fired the whole crew, except Hop High and Doc Lee. Me and Shorty Delmar went out there and had a talk with Slim about it, and this mornin' the law is goin' to take the boys back and take over the Circle C until you come home."

"Good! Oh, Red, that is fine! Until I come back?"

171

"Yea-a-ah, that's what they said."

Red's eyes roved around the broken walls and piled rubble. There was a wooden box, partly concealed in the rubble. He could see part of the black lettering, and the letters were DYNA—. Red drew a deep breath and turned to Dale.

"That box over there," he said meaningly. Dale nodded.

"They explained it to me," she said. "This place has been mined, Red. When they are through with it—" Dale hesitated.

"Yea-a-ah!" breathed Red. "I reckon I know what yuh mean. Well, it won't take much of a push."

"Does anybody know you came here?" asked Dale anxiously.

"Poison does. He's my pardner, Dale. If I don't come back, I'm afraid he'll come down here— mebbe alone."

"But why did they capture you, Red? You haven't anything to do with my troubles."

"Mebbe I was nosy." He grinned again.

They were silent for a while, and then Dale said:

"Who are you, Red?"

"Who am I? Why, I'm Red Blank, Dale. Don't yuh feel good?"

"I feel all right. I heard Slim Blake say, 'He can't fool me. I know who he is, and he's packing his father's gun.' "

"He said that?" queried Red.

"Yes. He said your name is Avery."

Red stared out at the shafts of sunlight against

the painted cliffs. In the sky, far above them, several buzzards floated on motionless wings.

"We're in a tough spot, Dale," Red said, "and this is no time for pardners to lie to each other. My name is Avery."

"I know," she said quietly. "I've heard my father talk about it—the robbery of the Aztec bank, and all that."

"Your father hated my father," said Red. "We were nesters. Do you know where my father and grandfather were buried, Dale?"

"Alex Trumbull showed me their graves, Red. The people didn't want them buried in the cemetery, so Alex cursed them all and had the bodies buried near his old ranch house. He made boards for them, too."

"I didn't know that, Dale. Old Alex Trumbull— I heard that yore dad hated Alex, because he tried to back my folks."

"Maybe," she said. "I don't know, Red. But that doesn't explain why they brought you here today."

"No, it don't. Mebbe I'm wrong, but I've got a hunch. We'll wait and see what happens."

Chapter 10
Death Bargain

It was a long day, and Red and Dale were very uncomfortable. The man had drawn the ropes tight, and Red's arms ached from retarded circulation. Dale said they had fed her a little, and given her water, but they never came that evening with any food.

The two dozed between talks, and it was close to midnight when they heard someone coming. One voice was whining, begging, as they shuffled along the ledge. There was a bright moon, and they saw David Sanders, herded in by Slim Blake.

The lawyer was scratched and bruised, and frightened to death. He collapsed on the floor, begging all the while to be taken home, while Slim roped his ankles.

"You'll stay here, you snivelin', yellow-backed

pup," snarled the big foreman of the Circle C.
"You'll stay here, until yuh tell me the truth."

"I've told you the truth!" wailed the lawyer.

"Well, how do yuh like it, you red pup?" asked
Slim.

"Fine," replied Red. "Nice place yuh selected
for us. What are yuh tryin' to do—move the town
down here, Slim?"

"Don't try to be funny."

"What's the idea of a lawyer?" asked Red.

"Sanders happens to know what the idea is.
Dale, are yuh ready to talk sense?"

"I have nothing to say," replied Dale firmly.

"You and Sanders will talk soon enough. No
food, no water from now on. And you'll talk, too,
Red."

"On what subject, Slim?" asked Red curiously.

"You ain't foolin' me, Red. I spotted yuh the
day yuh showed up. That six-shooter, with the
silver wolf head. Yore old man almost got me
with that gun one day."

"Too bad he missed," said Red soberly. "But
what's that got to do with me?"

"Don't know, eh? Well, I'll tell yuh somethin',
Red. That mornin' after the Aztec bank robbery,
you found the money and hid it. Don't deny it. We
found yore tracks in the dust—kid tracks. You
came back to dig it up—and that's what yo're
goin' to do, before I finish with yuh."

"That's interestin'," remarked Red calmly.
"Before yuh finish with me, eh? Meanin' that I
don't go back, eh?"

"That's the big idea. How do yuh like it?"

Red laughed at him. "Yo're an awful fool, Slim.

I heard about yore scheme to dump this shack into the canyon, after you've got all the information yuh need. If Dale is dead, what chance will you have to get the Circle C? None. If you dump me into the canyon with her, what chance do you have to get that money? None.

"You figure out a decent deal, a deal that we can go through with and have a chance for life. Otherwise, you'll get nothin', and merely add a few more murders to yore string."

"What do yuh mean?" asked Slim harshly.

"Check back on yore record, Slim."

"I wouldn't trust yuh, Red," Slim said, after a few moments of thought.

"All right. Touch off the fuse and go away broke, with the law only a jump behind yuh."

Slim's laugh held no conviction. "Nobody knows that any of yuh are here," he said.

"Keep on believin' that, Slim."

"You can't scare me. Tomorrow it'll be hot and you'll have no water. The next day it'll be hot— no water. If that don't work, did yuh ever see designs drawed on yore bare skin with a cigarette? Holes burned in yore eyelids? It's a lot of fun, makin' fools talk. Think it over."

Slim walked out and they heard him going up the rope ladder. David Sanders groaned painfully.

"And that man was one of my family for years, Red," Dale said.

"Yeah, that's right. Mebbe he's got Apache blood in him. He has such pleasant ideas."

"I haven't done anything wrong," wailed the

lawyer. "I've treated everybody right, and I've got friends, I tell you! I've got—"

"You've got a yellow streak right up yore spine," added Red.

"But I don't want to die!"

"Then why don't you tell him who opened yore safe?"

"I don't know, I tell you. He thinks I do know, but I don't."

"Slim used to be yore friend," said Red.

"He's a dirty crook! He wanted me to show him Hank Claybourn's will, but I never did it. He said he'd give me plenty to help him marry Dale. He said that I could help him, but I—I wouldn't."

"You wanted to marry her yourself, eh?" said Red.

"Who wouldn't?" asked Sanders flatly.

Dale laughed. In spite of her position in the matter, that remark struck her as being humorous. Red laughed, too.

"Slim swore that Dale hired somebody to steal that will," Sanders said. "You can't convince him of anything."

It was a mighty long night. Sanders complained unceasingly, trying to explain that it was all a mistake. Once in a while he prayed, too.

"Keep yore chin up, Dale," advised Red. "We ain't through yet."

It was nearly daylight when Slim Blake came again. Slim was worried. He admitted that men were searching for Sanders and Red, but had no idea that Dale was with them.

"I'm givin' yuh until dark to decide where that will is," he said. "And, Red, I want that money, too. I'll be back after dark, and you'll have an answer for me, or fifteen minutes after I leave here, this old bird's nest will fall into the canyon. It won't take much of a blast. Remember that, and get ready to talk fast. I'm savin' my own skin, even if I go away from here busted. *Adios*, you fools—until dark."

And then Slim Blake was gone in the chill of the false dawn.

"Well, that's plain enough," said Red. "Slim's scared, and a badman scared is the worst kind. He'll do anythin' to save his own skin. If we only had some food and water, it wouldn't be so bad."

"I don't want to die," quavered the lawyer. "I— I don't deserve to die. I ain't fit to die!"

"Even a lawyer gets around to tellin' the truth sooner or later," remarked Red dryly.

"You're not afraid, Red?" Dale asked quietly.

"Scared stiff, Dale. We're all scared. Nobody wants to die, because we don't know what's out there. Mebbe it's better than this, but I'll take my chances here."

"If we only knew where that will was!" complained the lawyer.

"What good would that do?" asked Red. "Slim can't afford to let us get away. He wouldn't last an hour, and he knows that."

"There must be some good in the man!" wailed Sanders.

"You try to find it," said Dale. "He's no good."

"I guess we are lost," said Sanders, his voice husky with fear.

"Yore opinion don't make it final," said Red.

The morning drifted on. Sunlight came through

the broken masonry. From where Red sat against the old wall he could still see that dynamite box. Dale looked miserable, and Red knew she was suffering. Sanders sprawled on some rubble, his face gray.

Red was staring down at his dirty clothes, his stringy old vest, and he suddenly had an idea.

"Dale," he said quietly. "Dale, I—I remember somethin'."

She lifted her head quickly. "What is it, Red?"

"A little pocket knife—such a little one," he whispered. "It was in my vest pocket. I always carried it there, but there was a hole, and it is inside the linin'. I meant to take it out, but didn't. If you could. . . . Wait! I'll slide over to yuh, Dale. Can yuh use yore fingers at all?"

"A little bit," she said. "My arms ache, but I think I can use them a little. But I can't see what you can do."

"Wait!" Red snaked his way over to her. "If you can sit on my lap, Dale, get close to me, mebbe you can feel it. We've got to try and get it."

"I'll try," she said. "I haven't much feeling in my body."

"Even if you had it—" began Sanders hopelessly.

"Stop that!" snapped Red. "Anyway it'll give us somethin' to do, except worry."

It was quite an ordeal for both Dale and Red, but after several attempts she was able to get on his lap, her hands close to the bottom of his old vest. Her fingers were cramped and numb, but she managed to discover that tiny knife in the lining of the vest. Tears ran down her cheeks, but she was game to the core, and finally was able to tear away the old lining and get that precious knife.

It fell from her fingers to the dirt, as she slid away. Red twisted around on his back and finally got the knife in his fingers. By twisting his hands in the knotted rope, he was able to open the little blade. Sanders watched Red finally accomplish the feat, and it gave him a ray of hope.

"Hold still, Dale!" panted Red. "I've got to back into yuh and see if I've got grip enough in my fingers to cut yore rope."

It was a long, tedious job, in which Red managed to drop the little knife several times, writhing around on his back to recover it again, but he finally sawed the strands of the hard rope, releasing her wrists. As soon as she was able to use her hands, it was no job to release both Red and Sanders.

They hobbled around, getting circulation into their legs, and working their arms to take out the stiffness. They were free, as far as the ropes were concerned, but there was only one way out of the old place, and the ropes were up there under that manzanita.

"We're no better off than before, Red," Sanders said. "They'll come down here and kill all of us. If they know we're loose, they'll dynamite us."

Red laughed at him, but the lawyer saw no humor in the situation.

There was not a lot of time left. Red climbed

up on the broken wall at the rear of the old dwelling and studied the face of the cliff. There was a broken fissure, extending up to another shelf, but it was at least twenty feet to that shelf, which might not lead to anything at all. The overhang up there prevented them from seeing what was beyond.

Red took off his boots and socks. Dale and Sanders watched him curiously, as he tightened his belt, his jaw tight, eyes studying the wall.

"What are you going to do, Red?" whispered Dale.

"Try to save three lives," he said tensely, and climbed back to the broken wall.

"You can't climb that!" blurted Sanders.

Red ignored him.

CHAPTER 11
"It's the Finish!"

RED WAS ALMOST AS PESSIMISTIC AS SANDERS, BUT he was willing to try anything now. He swayed in against the wall and searched for fingerholds. The wall was almost perpendicular, but that crevice gave him a chance to wedge his left elbow.

Slowly he went upward, toes digging for a tiny hold, his fingers clutching, shifting his elbow up and up, taking most of the weight. Ten feet, twelve feet.

Dale turned her eyes away, panting, suffering almost as much as Red. He was fairly lifting himself straight up. She flinched as a shower of small rocks clattered down.

"He's up to the ledge!" Sanders whispered.

Dale looked up. Red had his left elbow hooked over the ledge, his legs dangling away from the rock. He swung his right hand up and over the ledge, as a laugh broke the stillness. Dale and Sanders ran to the entrance. Up on that ledge by the manzanita was the masked man, with a rifle. He could see Red's head and shoulders above the ledge.

"So you got loose, eh?" he said. "Almost made it. Well, it's your funeral."

He lifted his rifle to his shoulder and laughed again as he cuddled the stock against his right jaw.

"No—no!" Dale screamed.

From somewhere came the sharp snap and the echoing report of a thirty-thirty, but it wasn't from the masked man's gun. The masked man had jerked forward, and fired his gun downward against the ledge, the bullet screaming far over Red's head. Then the masked man went down, striking on one knee, toppled off the ledge and went into Ghost Canyon, end over end.

Dale shut her eyes and leaned in against the broken wall.

"I made it!" Red called huskily. "I'll have to work my way around to that ledge. See yuh in a few minutes. Go out on the ledge and grab the ladder."

It was at least fifteen minutes before Red reached the manzanita. He tossed down the rope ladder and the loose rope.

"Tie the rope around under Dale's arms, Sanders," he called. "If she should slip on the ladder, she won't fall."

They were all exhausted when they reached the rim of the canyon. Red's elbows, knees and fingers were bleeding, but he didn't mind. The rough rocks of that climb had taken toll of him, but his grin was still there, doing business at the old stand.

They found the horse that the masked man had ridden, and they also found the horse that Red had hidden in a mesquite thicket. It was almost dark. Red put Dale on his horse and helped Sanders mount the other animal. Sanders was almost hysterical.

"Don't hug me!" exploded Red. "I hate to be hugged by a man."

"Do you draw the line on—on women, Red?" asked Dale.

"Do I . . . Gosh sakes, no! Dale!"

A minute later Sanders said, "There's a time for all things, I reckon. If that Slim Blake comes back . . . Look out!"

A man had stepped out from behind a rock, a rifle loose in his hands, and he was laughing. It was old Alex Trumbull.

"Alex!" exclaimed Red. "You—you fired that shot, the one that saved all of us!"

"Well, I heard him," chuckled the old man. "I've been pesticatin' around, kinda lookin' things over. I seen he was masked, and when a man wears a mask I start shootin'. What's this all about anyway?"

"Let's head for town," suggested the lawyer. "I don't like this place, and it's almost dark. We can tell you everything on the way."

"We'll ride double, Red," said the old man. "My bronc is over here a ways. . . ."

* * *

There was a crowd in the smoke-filled War Dance Saloon. Twenty men had just ridden in from a hard day of searching for Red and Sanders. It was still believed that Dale had gone away voluntarily. Shorty Delmar, the sheriff, Lonely Harte, Poison Oakes, and all the boys from the Circle C had been in that posse. The men had circled Ghost Canyon, but had been unable to find anybody.

Slim Blake was there, big, arrogant, triumphant. The will of Hank Claybourn was in the recorder's office, and Slim could afford to crow a little. He said he had found it at the ranch, and no one could contradict him.

"I'll buy everybody a drink," Slim said. "The Circle C belongs to me, and I'll run it to suit myself. Step up and have a—"

Slim's invitation stopped abruptly. Red Blank had stepped into the War Dance Saloon, and was coming slowly toward the bar. He was hatless, barefooted, blood was on his arms and hands, and his knees were showing through his torn overalls. There was blood on his face, too—blood and dirt. Around his waist was old Alex Trumbull's gun-belt, with Alex's black-handled Colt in the short holster.

"Red!" gasped Poison. "The ol' Red Feller is back!"

But Red had eyes only for Slim Blake, whose face was the color of wood ashes. Red stopped ten feet away and looked at Slim.

There was not a sound in the saloon, except for the heavy breathing.

Red's lips hardly moved, as he said:

"You failed, Slim. It's the finish."

Slim Blake was stunned, but game. He went for his gun, faster than most men can draw, but Red had been taught by Bill Keith, the old master gunslinger, and Slim's hand had barely smacked against his holster when Red's first bullet smashed his right shoulder. The draw was too fast to follow. The second bullet smashed almost into the same spot before Slim's muscles reacted to the shock of the first one.

Slim's gun clattered to the floor, he spun on his heels from the shock and went down, sprawling on his face. Men were dodging every way, upsetting chairs, tables. Red went slowly forward, kicked Slim's gun aside, and stood over him. Then he turned Slim over. The big man was not dead, but hit hard. Someone went for the doctor.

Slim blinked painfully at the circle of faces around him.

"The finish," he whispered. "Hurt—bad—I reckon."

"Bad enough, Slim," said Red. "You might as well talk. Yore pardner is down at the bottom of Ghost Canyon, full of lead. Nobody left for you to protect. You killed Hank Claybourn."

"Doc—Lee—gone?" Slim scowled painfully. "Nobody left? Yeah, I killed—Hank." Slim was spacing his words painfully. "Doc—is a—forger. Fooled—everybody. Give me a drink."

Someone handed him a glass of whisky, but had to pour it into his mouth. It seemed to revive Slim. He swallowed painfully.

"We stole Hank's will," he went on slowly,

"and Doc wrote a new one, after Hank was killed. I thought Dale and Sanders stole it. I had them dead to rights, and Doc wrote a new one yesterday—the one I filed. Hank left everything to Dale. It's hers—I won't need a ranch—where I'm— goin'."

Slim's eyes closed and they thought he had fainted, but Red didn't.

"Slim," he said, "you and Nick Little robbed the Aztec bank that time, and killed the banker. It wasn't my father and grandfather, Jim and Caleb Avery."

"We—robbed—it," said Slim. "It—wasn't— yore—folks." Slim roused momentarily and his voice was stronger, as he said: "You lied about Nick Little bein' a sheepherder in Wyomin'. I went into Ghost Canyon and found his bones."

"I know yuh did, Slim. Me and Poison saw yuh toss a marker into the canyon."

"You—knew—too—much," whispered Slim. "Tell—Dale I'm—sorry."

"He's fainted," said Shorty Delmar.

"Call it that, if yuh want to," said a cowboy. "I think it's permanent."

"Well, dog my cats!" exploded Lonely. "Old Alex is cleared!"

The men nodded soberly. Red walked out as the doctor came in. He found Dale, Alex and Sanders across the street, and Poison was telling them what had happened. Old Alex was doing a double shuffle on the sidewalk, and Dale was crying. Red took her in his arms, and Poison stood there, his mouth wide.

"What do yuh think of that, Poison?" asked Alex Trumbull.

"Not much," whispered Poison soberly. "Me and him have been together for years, and I thought he was female proof, but doggone it, he's busted the set."

"I forgot somethin'," said Red. "When I crawled over the top of that old dwellin', tryin' to get back to that ledge, I shoved a flat rock aside and I found the money I hid there twelve years ago. It's all right, I believe. It belongs to the Aztec bank."

"That's what I don't like about love," said Poison soberly.

"What's that?" asked Sanders.

"It makes yuh too danged honest."

"Yuh see," Red was explaining to Dale, "Slim figured that you and Sanders were the only ones who knew where that will was, so after he got both of yuh into the canyon, he had Doc Lee make another copy. All he had to do was touch off the blast, and collect the Circle C."

"But it doesn't make sense, Red," protested Sanders. "Neither Dale nor I know where that other will is. There's a third party in on this, and if Doc Lee made another copy, it couldn't have been him."

Red laughed quietly, and Dale understood.

"Red, you—you got it?" she said softly.

Red didn't deny it. He put his arm around her.

"Alex, this ain't no place for ol' rannahans like me and you," Poison said. "I'll buy yuh a drink."

"I'll drink it," replied Alex shortly.